Three Short Works

Three Short Works

Gustave Flaubert

MINT EDITIONS

Three Short Works was first published in 1877.

This edition published by Mint Editions 2021.

ISBN 9781513279510 | E-ISBN 9781513284538

Published by Mint Editions®

MINT
EDITIONS

minteditionbooks.com

Publishing Director: Jennifer Newens
Design & Production: Rachel Lopez Metzger
Project Manager: Micaela Clark
Typesetting: Westchester Publishing Services

Contents

THE DANCE OF DEATH

(1838)

"Many words for few things!"
"Death ends all; judgment comes to all."

(This work may be called a prose poem. It is impregnated with the spirit of romanticism, which at the time of writing had a temporary but powerful hold on the mind of Gustave Flaubert.)

Death Speaks

At night, in winter, when the snow-flakes fall slowly from heaven like great white tears, I raise my voice; its resonance thrills the cypress trees and makes them bud anew.

I pause an instant in my swift course over earth; throw myself down among cold tombs; and, while dark-plumaged birds rise suddenly in terror from my side, while the dead slumber peacefully, while cypress branches droop low o'er my head, while all around me weeps or lies in deep repose, my burning eyes rest on the great white clouds, gigantic winding-sheets, unrolling their slow length across the face of heaven.

How many nights, and years, and ages have I journeyed thus! A witness of the universal birth and of a like decay; Innumerable are the generations I have garnered with my scythe. Like God, I am eternal! The nurse of Earth, I cradle it each night upon a bed both soft and warm. The same recurring feasts; the same unending toil! Each morning I depart, each evening I return, bearing within my mantle's ample folds all that my scythe has gathered. And then I scatter them to the four winds of Heaven!

When the high billows run, when the heavens weep, and shrieking winds lash ocean into madness, then in the turmoil and the tumult do I fling myself upon the surging waves, and lo! the tempest softly cradles me, as in her hammock sways a queen. The foaming waters cool my weary feet, burning from bathing in the falling tears of countless generations that have clung to them in vain endeavour to arrest my steps.

Then, when the storm has ceased, after its roar has calmed me like a lullaby, I bow my head: the hurricane, raging in fury but a moment earlier dies instantly. No longer does it live, but neither do the men, the ships, the navies that lately sailed upon the bosom of the waters.

'Mid all that I have seen and known,—peoples and thrones, loves, glories, sorrows, virtues—what have I ever loved? Nothing—except the mantling shroud that covers me!

My horse! ah, yes! my horse! I love thee too! How thou rushest o'er the world! thy hoofs of steel resounding on the heads bruised by thy speeding feet. Thy tail is straight and crisp, thine eyes dart flames, the mane upon thy neck flies in the wind, as on we dash upon our maddened course. Never art thou weary! Never do we rest! Never do we sleep! Thy neighing portends war; thy smoking nostrils spread a pestilence that, mist-like, hovers over earth. Where'er my arrows fly, thou overturnest pyramids and empires, trampling crowns beneath thy hoofs; All men respect thee; nay, adore thee! To invoke thy favour, popes offer thee their triple crowns, and kings their sceptres; peoples, their secret sorrows; poets, their renown. All cringe and kneel before thee, yet thou rushest on over their prostrate forms.

Ah, noble steed! Sole gift from heaven! Thy tendons are of iron, thy head is of bronze. Thou canst pursue thy course for centuries as swiftly as if borne up by eagle's wings; and when, once in a thousand years, resistless hunger comes, thy food is human flesh, thy drink, men's tears. My steed! I love thee as Pale Death alone can love!

Ah! I have lived so long! How many things I know! How many mysteries of the universe are shut within my breast!

Sometimes, after I have hurled a myriad of darts, and, after coursing o'er the world on my pale horse, have gathered many lives, a weariness assails me, and I long to rest.

But on my work must go; my path I must pursue; it leads through infinite space and all the worlds. I sweep away men's plans together with their triumphs, their loves together with their crimes, their very all.

I rend my winding-sheet; a frightful craving tortures me incessantly, as if some serpent stung continually within.

I throw a backward glance, and see the smoke of fiery ruins left behind; the darkness of the night; the agony of the world. I see the graves that are the work of these, my hands; I see the background of the past—'tis nothingness! My weary body, heavy head, and tired feet, sink, seeking rest. My eyes turn towards a glowing horizon, boundless, immense, seeming to grow increasingly in height and depth. I shall devour it, as I have devoured all else.

When, O God! shall I sleep in my turn? When wilt Thou cease creating? When may I, digging my own grave, stretch myself out within my tomb, and, swinging thus upon the world, list the last breath, the death-gasp, of expiring nature?

When that time comes, away my darts and shroud I'll hurl. Then shall I free my horse, and he shall graze upon the grass that grows upon the Pyramids, sleep in the palaces of emperors, drink the last drop of water from the sea, and snuff the odour of the last slow drop of blood!

By day, by night, through the countless ages, he shall roam through fields eternal as the fancy takes him; shall leap with one great bound from Atlas to the Himalayas; shall course, in his insolent pride, from heaven to earth; disport himself by caracoling in the dust of crumbled empires; shall speed across the beds of dried-up oceans; shall bound o'er ruins of enormous cities; inhale the void with swelling chest, and roll and stretch at ease.

Then haply, faithful one, weary as I, thou finally shalt seek some precipice from which to cast thyself; shalt halt, panting before the mysterious ocean of infinity; and then, with foaming mouth, dilated nostrils, and extended neck turned towards the horizon, thou shalt, as I, pray for eternal sleep; for repose for thy fiery feet; for a bed of green leaves, whereon reclining thou canst close thy burning eyes forever. There, waiting motionless upon the brink, thou shalt desire a power stronger than thyself to kill thee at a single blow—shalt pray for union with the dying storm, the faded flower, the shrunken corpse. Thou shalt seek sleep, because eternal life is torture, and the tomb is peace.

Why are we here? What hurricane has hurled us into this abyss? What tempest soon shall bear us away towards the forgotten planets whence we came?

Till then, my glorious steed, thou shalt run thy course; thou mayst please thine ear with the crunching of the heads crushed under thy feet. Thy course is long, but courage! Long time hast thou carried me: but longer time still must elapse, and yet we shall not age.

Stars may be quenched, the mountains crumble, the earth finally wear away its diamond axis; but we two, we alone are immortal, for the impalpable lives forever!

But to-day them canst lie at my feet, and polish thy teeth against the moss-grown tombs, for Satan has abandoned me, and a power unknown compels me to obey his will. Lo! the dead seek to rise from their graves.

SATAN, I LOVE THEE! THOU alone canst comprehend my joys and my deliriums. But, more fortunate than I, thou wilt some day, when earth shall be no more, recline and sleep within the realms of space.

But I, who have lived so long, have worked so ceaselessly, with only virtuous loves and solemn thoughts,—I must endure immortality. Man has his tomb, and glory its oblivion; the day dies into night but I—!

And I am doomed to lasting solitude upon my way, strewn with the bones of men and marked by ruins. Angels have fellow-angels; demons their companions of darkness; but I hear only sounds of a clanking scythe, my whistling arrows, and my speeding horse. Always the echo of the surging billows that sweep over and engulf mankind!

SATAN: Dost thou complain,—thou, the most fortunate creature under heaven? The only, splendid, great, unchangeable, eternal one—like God, who is the only Being that equals thee! Dost thou repine, who some day in thy turn shalt disappear forever, after thou hast crushed the universe beneath thy horse's feet?

When God's work of creating has ceased; when the heavens have disappeared and the stars are quenched; when spirits rise from their retreats and wander in the depths with sighs and groans; then, what unpicturable delight for thee! Then shalt thou sit on the eternal thrones of heaven and of hell—shalt overthrow the planets, stars, and worlds—shalt loose thy steed in fields of emeralds and diamonds—shalt make his litter of the wings torn from the angels,—shalt cover him with the robe of righteousness! Thy saddle shall be broidered with the stars of the empyrean,—and then thou wilt destroy it! After thou hast annihilated everything,—when naught remains but empty space,—thy coffin shattered and thine arrows broken, then make thyself a crown of stone from heaven's highest mount, and cast thyself into the abyss of oblivion. Thy fall may last a million aeons, but thou shalt die at last. Because the world must end; all, all must die,—except Satan! Immortal more than God! I live to bring chaos into other worlds!

DEATH: But thou hast not, as I, this vista of eternal nothingness before thee; thou dost not suffer with this death-like cold, as I.

SATAN: Nay, but I quiver under fierce and unrelaxing hearts of molten lava, which burn the doomed and which e'en I cannot escape.

For thou, at least, hast only to destroy. But I bring birth and I give life. I direct empires and govern the affairs of States and of hearts.

I must be everywhere. The precious metals flow, the diamonds glitter, and men's names resound at my command. I whisper in the ears of women, of poets, and of statesmen, words of love, of glory, of ambition. With Messalina and Nero, at Paris and at Babylon, within the self-same moment do I dwell. Let a new island be discovered, I fly to it ere man can set foot there; though it be but a rock encircled by the sea, I am there in advance of men who will dispute for its possession. I lounge, at the same instant, on a courtesan's couch and on the perfumed beds of emperors. Hatred and envy, pride and wrath, pour from my lips in simultaneous utterance. By night and day I work. While men ate burning Christians, I luxuriate voluptuously in baths perfumed with roses; I race in chariots; yield to deep despair; or boast aloud in pride.

At times I have believed that I embodied the whole world, and all that I have seen took place, in verity, within my being.

Sometimes I weary, lose my reason, and indulge in such mad follies that the most worthless of my minions ridicule me while they pity me.

No creature cares for me; nowhere am I loved,—neither in heaven, of which I am a son, nor yet in hell, where I am lord, nor upon earth, where men deem me a god. Naught do I see but paroxysms of rage, rivers of blood, or maddened frenzy. Ne'er shall my eyelids close in slumber, never my spirit find repose, whilst thou, at least, canst rest thy head upon the cool, green freshness of the grave. Yea, I must ever dwell amid the glare of palaces, must listen to the curses of the starving, or inhale the stench of crimes that cry aloud to heaven.

God, whom I hate, has punished me indeed! But my soul is greater even than His wrath; in one deep sigh I could the whole world draw into my breast, where it would burn eternally, even as I.

When, Lord, shall thy great trumpet sound? Then a great harmony shall hover over sea and hill. Ah! would that I could suffer with humanity; their cries and sobs should drown the sound of mine!

(*Innumerable skeletons, riding in chariots, advance at a rapid pace, with cries of joy and triumph. They drag broken branches and crowns of laurel, from which the dried and yellow leaves fall continually in the wind and the dust*)

Lo, a triumphal throng from Rome, the Eternal City! Her Coliseum and her Capitol are now two grains of sands that served once as a pedestal; but Death has swung his scythe: the monuments have fallen. Behold! At their head comes Nero, pride of my heart, the greatest poet earth has known!

(*Nero advances in a chariot drawn by twelve skeleton horses. With the sceptre in his hand, he strikes the bony backs of his steeds. He stands erect, his shroud flapping behind him in billowy folds. He turns, as if upon a racecourse; his eyes are flaming and he cries loudly:*)

NERO: Quick! Quick! And faster still, until your feet dash fire from the flinty stones and your nostrils fleck your breasts with foam. What! do not the wheels smoke yet? Hear ye the fanfares, whose sound reached even to Ostia; the clapping of the hands, the cries of joy? See how the populace shower saffron on my head! See how my pathway is already damp with sprayed perfume! My chariot whirls on; the pace is swifter than the wind as I shake the golden reins! Faster and faster! The dust clouds rise; my mantle floats upon the breeze, which in my ears sings "Triumph! triumph!" Faster and faster! Hearken to the shouts of joy, list to the stamping feet and the plaudits of the multitude. Jupiter himself looks down on us from heaven. Faster! yea, faster still!

(*Nero's chariot now seems to be drawn by demons: a black cloud of dust and smoke envelops him; in his erratic course he crashes into tombs, and the re-awakened corpses are crushed under the wheels of the chariot, which now turns, comes forward, and stops*)

NERO: Now, let six hundred of my women dance the Grecian Dances silently before me, the while I lave myself with roses in a bath of porphyry. Then let them circle me, with interlacing arms, that I may see on all sides alabaster forms in graceful evolution, swaying like tall reeds bending over an amorous pool.

And I will give the empire and the sea, the Senate, the Olympus, the Capitol, to her who shall embrace me the most ardently; to her whose heart shall throb beneath my own; to her who shall enmesh me in her flowing hair, smile on me sweetest, and enfold me in the warmest clasp; to her who soothing me with songs of love shall waken me to joy and heights of rapture! Rome shall be still this night; no barque shall cleave the waters of the Tiber, since 'tis my wish to see the mirrored moon on its untroubled face and hear the voice of woman floating over it. Let perfumed breezes pass through all my draperies! Ah, I would die, voluptuously intoxicated.

Then, while I eat of some rare meat, that only I may taste, let some one sing, while damsels, lightly draped, serve me from plates of gold and watch my rest. One slave shall cut her sister's throat, because it is my pleasure—a favourite with the gods—to mingle the perfume of blood with that of food, and cries of victims soothe my nerves.

This night I shall burn Rome. The flames shall light up heaven, and Tiber shall roll in waves of fire!

Then, I shall build of aloes wood a stage to float upon the Italian sea, and the Roman populace shall throng thereto chanting my praise. Its draperies shall be of purple, and on it I shall have a bed of eagles' plumage. There I shall sit, and at my side shall be the loveliest woman in the empire, while all the universe applauds the achievements of a god! And though the tempest roar round me, its rage shall be extinguished 'neath my feet, and sounds of music shall o'ercome the clamor of the waves!

* * * * *

What didst thou say? Vindex revolts, my legions fly, my women flee in terror? Silence and tears alone remain, and I hear naught but the rolling of thunder. Must I die, now?

DEATH: Instantly!

NERO: Must I give up my days of feasting and delight, my spectacles, my triumphs, my chariots and the applause of multitudes?

DEATH: All! All!

SATAN: Haste, Master of the World! One comes—One who will put thee to the sword. An emperor knows how to die!

NERO: Die! I have scarce begun to live! Oh, what great deeds I should accomplish—deeds that should make Olympus tremble! I would fill up the bed of hoary ocean and speed across it in a triumphal car. I would still live—would see the sun once more, the Tiber, the Campagna, the Circus on the golden sands. Ah! let me live!

Death: I will give thee a mantle for the tomb, and an eternal bed that shall be softer and more peaceful than the Imperial couch.

Nero: Yet, I am loth to die.

Death: Die, then!

(*He gathers up the shroud, lying beside him on the ground, and bears away Nero—wrapped in its folds*)

THE LEGEND OF SAINT JULIAN THE HOSPITALLER

I

The Curse

Julian's father and mother dwelt in a castle built on the slope of a hill, in the heart of the woods.

The towers at its four corners had pointed roofs covered with leaden tiles, and the foundation rested upon solid rocks, which descended abruptly to the bottom of the moat.

In the courtyard, the stone flagging was as immaculate as the floor of a church. Long rain-spouts, representing dragons with yawning jaws, directed the water towards the cistern, and on each window-sill of the castle a basil or a heliotrope bush bloomed, in painted flower-pots.

A second enclosure, surrounded by a fence, comprised a fruit-orchard, a garden decorated with figures wrought in bright-hued flowers, an arbour with several bowers, and a mall for the diversion of the pages. On the other side were the kennel, the stables, the bakery, the wine-press and the barns. Around these spread a pasture, also enclosed by a strong hedge.

Peace had reigned so long that the portcullis was never lowered; the moats were filled with water; swallows built their nests in the cracks of the battlements, and as soon as the sun shone too strongly, the archer who all day long paced to and fro on the curtain, withdrew to the watch-tower and slept soundly.

Inside the castle, the locks on the doors shone brightly; costly tapestries hung in the apartments to keep out the cold; the closets overflowed with linen, the cellar was filled with casks of wine, and the oak chests fairly groaned under the weight of money-bags.

In the armoury could be seen, between banners and the heads of wild beasts, weapons of all nations and of all ages, from the slings of the Amalekites and the javelins of the Garamantes, to the broad-swords of the Saracens and the coats of mail of the Normans.

The largest spit in the kitchen could hold an ox; the chapel was as gorgeous as a king's oratory. There was even a Roman bath in a secluded part of the castle, though the good lord of the manor refrained from using it, as he deemed it a heathenish practice.

Wrapped always in a cape made of fox-skins, he wandered about the castle, rendered justice among his vassals and settled his neighbours' quarrels. In the winter, he gazed dreamily at the falling snow, or had stories read aloud to him. But as soon as the fine weather returned, he would mount his mule and sally forth into the country roads, edged with ripening wheat, to talk with the peasants, to whom he distributed advice. After a number of adventures he took unto himself a wife of high lineage.

She was pale and serious, and a trifle haughty. The horns of her head-dress touched the top of the doors and the hem of her gown trailed far behind her. She conducted her household like a cloister. Every morning she distributed work to the maids, supervised the making of preserves and unguents, and afterwards passed her time in spinning, or in embroidering altar-cloths. In response to her fervent prayers, God granted her a son!

Then there was great rejoicing; and they gave a feast which lasted three days and four nights, with illuminations and soft music. Chickens as large as sheep, and the rarest spices were served; for the entertainment of the guests, a dwarf crept out of a pie; and when the bowls were too few, for the crowd swelled continuously, the wine was drunk from helmets and hunting-horns.

The young mother did not appear at the feast. She was quietly resting in bed. One night she awoke, and beheld in a moonbeam that crept through the window something that looked like a moving shadow. It was an old man clad in sackcloth, who resembled a hermit. A rosary dangled at his side and he carried a beggar's sack on his shoulder. He approached the foot of the bed, and without opening his lips said: "Rejoice, O mother! Thy son shall be a saint."

She would have cried out, but the old man, gliding along the moonbeam, rose through the air and disappeared. The songs of the banqueters grew louder. She could hear angels' voices, and her head sank back on the pillow, which was surmounted by the bone of a martyr, framed in precious stones.

The following day, the servants, upon being questioned, declared, to a man, that they had seen no hermit. Then, whether dream or fact, this must certainly have been a communication from heaven; but she took care not to speak of it, lest she should be accused of presumption.

The guests departed at daybreak, and Julian's father stood at the castle gate, where he had just bidden farewell to the last one, when a beggar suddenly emerged from the mist and confronted him. He was a gipsy—for he had a braided beard and wore silver bracelets on each arm. His eyes burned and, in an inspired way, he muttered some disconnected words: "Ah! Ah! thy son!—great bloodshed—great glory—happy always—an emperor's family."

Then he stooped to pick up the alms thrown to him, and disappeared in the tall grass.

The lord of the manor looked up and down the road and called as loudly as he could. But no one answered him! The wind only howled and the morning mists were fast dissolving.

He attributed his vision to a dullness of the brain resulting from too much sleep. "If I should speak of it," quoth he, "people would laugh at me." Still, the glory that was to be his son's dazzled him, albeit the meaning of the prophecy was not clear to him, and he even doubted that he had heard it.

The parents kept their secret from each other. But both cherished the child with equal devotion, and as they considered him marked by God, they had great regard for his person. His cradle was lined with the softest feathers, and lamp representing a dove burned continually over it; three nurses rocked him night and day, and with his pink cheeks and blue eyes, brocaded cloak and embroidered cap he looked like a little Jesus. He cut all his teeth without even a whimper.

When he was seven years old his mother taught him to sing, and his father lifted him upon a tall horse, to inspire him with courage. The child smiled with delight, and soon became familiar with everything pertaining to chargers. An old and very learned monk taught him the Gospel, the Arabic numerals, the Latin letters, and the art of painting delicate designs on vellum. They worked in the top of a tower, away from all noise and disturbance.

When the lesson was over, they would go down into the garden and study the flowers.

Sometimes a herd of cattle passed through the valley below, in charge of a man in Oriental dress. The lord of the manor, recognising him as a merchant, would despatch a servant after him. The stranger, becoming confident, would stop on his way and after being ushered into the castle-hall, would display pieces of velvet and silk, trinkets and strange objects whose use was unknown in those parts. Then, in due time, he would take leave, without having been molested and with a handsome profit.

At other times, a band of pilgrims would knock at the door. Their wet garments would be hung in front of the hearth and after they had been refreshed by food they would relate their travels, and discuss the uncertainty of vessels on the high seas, their long journeys across burning sands, the ferocity of the infidels, the caves of Syria, the Manger and the Holy Sepulchre. They made presents to the young heir of beautiful shells, which they carried in their cloaks.

The lord of the manor very often feasted his brothers-at-arms, and over the wine the old warriors would talk of battles and attacks, of war-machines and of the frightful wounds they had received, so that Julian, who was a listener, would scream with excitement; then his father felt convinced that some day he would be a conqueror. But in the evening, after the Angelus, when he passed through the crowd of beggars who clustered about the church-door, he distributed his alms with so much modesty and nobility that his mother fully expected to see him become an archbishop in time.

His seat in the chapel was next to his parents, and no matter how long the services lasted, he remained kneeling on his *prie-dieu,* with folded hands and his velvet cap lying close beside him on the floor.

One day, during mass, he raised his head and beheld a little white mouse crawling out of a hole in the wall. It scrambled to the first altar-step and then, after a few gambols, ran back in the same direction. On the following Sunday, the idea of seeing the mouse again worried him. It returned; and every Sunday after that he watched for it; and it annoyed him so much that he grew to hate it and resolved to do away with it.

So, having closed the door and strewn some crumbs on the steps of the altar, he placed himself in front of the hole with a stick. After a long while a pink snout appeared, and then whole mouse crept out. He struck it lightly with his stick and stood stunned at the sight of the little, lifeless body. A drop of blood stained the floor. He wiped it away hastily with his sleeve, and picking up the mouse, threw it away, without saying a word about it to anyone.

All sorts of birds pecked at the seeds in the garden. He put some peas in a hollow reed, and when he heard birds chirping in a tree, he would approach cautiously, lift the tube and swell his cheeks; then, when the little creatures dropped about him in multitudes, he could not refrain from laughing and being delighted with his own cleverness.

One morning, as he was returning by way of the curtain, he beheld a fat pigeon sunning itself on the top of the wall. He paused to gaze at it; where he stood the rampart was cracked and a piece of stone was near at hand; he gave his arm a jerk and the well-aimed missile struck the bird squarely, sending it straight into the moat below.

He sprang after it, unmindful of the brambles, and ferreted around the bushes with the litheness of a young dog.

The pigeon hung with broken wings in the branches of a privet hedge.

The persistence of its life irritated the boy. He began to strangle it, and its convulsions made his heart beat quicker, and filled him with a wild, tumultuous voluptuousness, the last throb of its heart making him feel like fainting.

At supper that night, his father declared that at his age a boy should begin to hunt; and he arose and brought forth an old writing-book which contained, in questions and answers, everything pertaining to the pastime. In it, a master showed a supposed pupil how to train dogs and falcons, lay traps, recognise a stag by its fumets, and a fox or a wolf by footprints. He also taught the best way of discovering their tracks, how to start them, where their refuges are usually to be found, what winds are the most favourable, and further enumerated the various cries, and the rules of the quarry.

When Julian was able to recite all these things by heart, his father made up a pack of hounds for him. There were twenty-four greyhounds of Barbary, speedier than gazelles, but liable to get out of temper; seventeen couples of Breton dogs, great barkers, with broad chests and russet coats flecked with white. For wild-boar hunting and perilous doublings, there were forty boarhounds as hairy as bears.

The red mastiffs of Tartary, almost as large as donkeys, with broad backs and straight legs, were destined for the pursuit of the wild bull. The black coats of the spaniels shone like satin; the barking of the setters equalled that of the beagles. In a special enclosure were eight growling bloodhounds that tugged at their chains and rolled their eyes, and these dogs leaped at men's throats and were not afraid even of lions.

All ate wheat bread, drank from marble troughs, and had high-sounding names.

Perhaps the falconry surpassed the pack; for the master of the castle, by paying great sums of money, had secured Caucasian hawks, Babylonian sakers, German gerfalcons, and pilgrim falcons captured on the cliffs edging the cold seas, in distant lands. They were housed in a thatched shed and were chained to the perch in the order of size. In front of them was a little grass-plot where, from time to time, they were allowed to disport themselves.

Bag-nets, baits, traps and all sorts of snares were manufactured.

Often they would take out pointers who would set almost immediately; then the whippers-in, advancing step by step, would cautiously spread a huge net over their motionless bodies. At the command, the dogs would bark and arouse the quails; and the ladies of the neighbourhood, with their husbands, children and hand-maids, would fall upon them and capture them with ease.

At other times they used a drum to start hares; and frequently foxes fell into the ditches prepared for them, while wolves caught their paws in the traps.

But Julian scorned these convenient contrivances; he preferred to hunt away from the crowd, alone with his steed and his falcon. It was almost always a large, snow-white, Scythian bird. His leather hood was ornamented with a plume, and on his blue feet were bells; and he perched firmly on his master's arm while they galloped across the plains. Then Julian would suddenly untie his tether and let him fly, and the bold bird would dart through the air like an arrow, One might perceive two spots circle around, unite, and then disappear in the blue heights. Presently the falcon would return with a mutilated bird, and perch again on his master's gauntlet with trembling wings.

Julian loved to sound his trumpet and follow his dogs over hills and streams, into the woods; and when the stag began to moan under their teeth, he would kill it deftly, and delight in the fury of the brutes, which would devour the pieces spread out on the warm hide.

On foggy days, he would hide in the marshes to watch for wild geese, otters and wild ducks.

At daybreak, three equerries waited for him at the foot of the steps; and though the old monk leaned out of the dormer-window and made signs to him to return, Julian would not look around.

He heeded neither the broiling sun, the rain nor the storm; he drank spring water and ate wild berries, and when he was tired, he lay down under a tree; and he would come home at night covered with earth and blood, with thistles in his hair and smelling of wild beasts. He grew to be like them. And when his mother kissed him, he responded coldly to her caress and seemed to be thinking of deep and serious things.

He killed bears with a knife, bulls with a hatchet, and wild boars with a spear; and once, with nothing but a stick, he defended himself against some wolves, which were gnawing corpses at the foot of a gibbet.

One winter morning he set out before daybreak, with a bow slung across his shoulder and a quiver of arrows attached to the pummel of his saddle. The hoofs of his steed beat the ground with regularity and his two beagles trotted close behind. The wind was blowing hard and icicles clung to his cloak. A part of the horizon cleared, and he beheld some rabbits playing around their burrows. In an instant, the two dogs were upon them, and seizing as many as they could, they broke their backs in the twinkling of an eye.

Soon he came to a forest. A woodcock, paralysed by the cold, perched on a branch, with its head hidden under its wing. Julian, with a lunge of his sword, cut off its feet, and without stopping to pick it up, rode away.

Three hours later he found himself on the top of a mountain so high that the sky seemed almost black. In front of him, a long, flat rock hung over a precipice, and at the end two wild goats stood gazing down into the abyss. As he had no arrows (for he had left his steed behind), he thought he would climb down to where they stood; and with bare feet and bent back he at last reached the first goat and thrust his dagger below its ribs. But the second animal, in its terror, leaped into the precipice. Julian threw himself forward to strike it, but his right foot slipped, and he fell, face downward and with outstretched arms, over the body of the first goat.

After he returned to the plains, he followed a stream bordered by willows. From time to time, some cranes, flying low, passed over his head. He killed them with his whip, never missing a bird. He beheld in the distance the gleam of a lake which appeared to be of lead, and in the middle of it was an animal he had never seen before, a beaver with a black muzzle. Notwithstanding the distance that separated them, an arrow ended its life and Julian only regretted that he was not able to carry the skin home with him.

Then he entered an avenue of tall trees, the tops of which formed a triumphal arch to the entrance of a forest. A deer sprang out of the thicket and a badger crawled out of its hole, a stag appeared in the road, and a peacock spread its fan-shaped tail on the grass—and after he had slain them all, other deer, other stags, other badgers, other peacocks, and jays, blackbirds, foxes, porcupines, polecats, and lynxes, appeared; in fact, a host of beasts that grew more and more numerous with every step he took. Trembling, and with a look of appeal in their eyes, they gathered around Julian, but he did not stop slaying them; and so intent was he on stretching his bow, drawing his sword and whipping out his knife, that he had little thought for aught else. He knew that he was hunting in some country since an indefinite time, through the very fact of his existence, as everything seemed to occur with the ease one experiences in dreams. But presently an extraordinary sight made him pause.

He beheld a valley shaped like a circus and filled with stags which, huddled together, were warming one another with the vapour of their breaths that mingled with the early mist.

For a few minutes, he almost choked with pleasure at the prospect of so great a carnage. Then he sprang from his horse, rolled up his sleeves, and began to aim.

When the first arrow whizzed through the air, the stags turned their heads simultaneously. They huddled closer, uttered plaintive cries, and a great agitation seized the whole herd. The edge of the valley was too high to admit of flight; and the animals ran around the enclosure in their efforts to escape. Julian aimed, stretched his bow and his arrows fell as fast and thick as raindrops in a shower.

Maddened with terror, the stags fought and reared and climbed on top of one another; their antlers and bodies formed a moving mountain which tumbled to pieces whenever it displaced itself. Finally the last one expired. Their bodies lay stretched out on the sand with foam gushing from the nostrils and the bowels protruding. The heaving of their bellies grew less and less noticeable, and presently all was still.

Night came, and behind the trees, through the branches, the sky appeared like a sheet of blood.

Julian leaned against a tree and gazed with dilated eyes at the enormous slaughter. He was now unable to comprehend how he had accomplished it.

On the opposite side of the valley, he suddenly beheld a large stag, with a doe and their fawn. The buck was black and of enormous size; he had a white beard and carried sixteen antlers. His mate was the color of dead leaves, and she browsed upon the grass, while the fawn, clinging to her udder, followed her step by step.

Again the bow was stretched, and instantly the fawn dropped dead, and seeing this, its mother raised her head and uttered a poignant, almost human wail of agony. Exasperated, Julian thrust his knife into her chest, and felled her to the ground.

The great stag had watched everything and suddenly he sprang forward. Julian aimed his last arrow at the beast. It struck him between his antlers and stuck there.

The stag did not appear to notice it; leaping over the bodies, he was coming nearer and nearer with the intention, Julian thought, of charging at him and ripping him open, and he recoiled with inexpressible horror. But presently the huge animal halted, and, with eyes aflame and the solemn air of a patriarch and a judge, repeated thrice, while a bell tolled in the distance: "Accursed! Accursed! Accursed! some day, ferocious soul, thou wilt murder thy father and thy mother!"

Then he sank on his knees, gently closed his lids and expired.

At first Julian was stunned, and then a sudden lassitude and an immense sadness came over him. Holding his head between his hands, he wept for a long time.

His steed had wandered away; his dogs had forsaken him; the solitude seemed to threaten him with unknown perils. Impelled by a sense of sickening terror, he ran across the fields, and choosing a path at random, found himself almost immediately at the gates of the castle.

That night he could not rest, for, by the flickering light of the hanging lamp, he beheld again the huge black stag. He fought against the obsession of the prediction and kept repeating: "No! No! No! I cannot slay them!" and then he thought: "Still, supposing I desired to?—" and he feared that the devil might inspire him with this desire.

During three months, his distracted mother prayed at his bedside, and his father paced the halls of the castle in anguish. He consulted the most celebrated physicians, who prescribed quantities of medicine. Julian's illness, they declared, was due to some injurious wind or to amorous desire. But in reply to their questions, the young man only shook his head. After a time, his strength returned, and he was able to take a walk in the courtyard, supported by his father and the old monk.

But after he had completely recovered, he refused to hunt.

His father, hoping to please him, presented him with a large Saracen sabre. It was placed on a panoply that hung on a pillar, and a ladder was required to reach it. Julian climbed up to it one day, but the heavy weapon slipped from his grasp, and in falling grazed his father and tore his cloak. Julian, believing he had killed him, fell in a swoon.

After that, he carefully avoided weapons. The sight of a naked sword made him grow pale, and this weakness caused great distress to his family.

In the end, the old monk ordered him in the name of God, and of his forefathers, once more to indulge in the sport's of a nobleman.

The equerries diverted themselves every day with javelins and Julian soon excelled in the practice.

He was able to send a javelin into bottles, to break the teeth of the weather-cocks on the castle and to strike door-nails at a distance of one hundred feet.

One summer evening, at the hour when dusk renders objects indistinct, he was in the arbour in the garden, and thought he saw two white wings in the background hovering around the espalier. Not for a moment did he doubt that it was a stork, and so he threw his javelin at it.

A heart-rending scream pierced the air.

He had struck his mother, whose cap and long streams remained nailed to the wall.

Julian fled from home and never returned.

II

The Crime

He joined a horde of adventurers who were passing through the place.

He learned what it was to suffer hunger, thirst, sickness and filth. He grew accustomed to the din of battles and to the sight of dying men. The wind tanned his skin. His limbs became hardened through contact with armour, and as he was very strong and brave, temperate and of good counsel, he easily obtained command of a company.

At the outset of a battle, he would electrify his soldiers by a motion of his sword. He would climb the walls of a citadel with a knotted rope, at night, rocked by the storm, while sparks of fire clung to his cuirass, and molten lead and boiling tar poured from the battlements.

Often a stone would break his shield. Bridges crowded with men gave way under him. Once, by turning his mace, he rid himself of fourteen horsemen. He defeated all those who came forward to fight him on the field of honour, and more than a score of times it was believed that he had been killed.

However, thanks to Divine protection, he always escaped, for he shielded orphans, widows, and aged men. When he caught sight of one of the latter walking ahead of him, he would call to him to show his face, as if he feared that he might kill him by mistake.

All sorts of intrepid men gathered under his leadership, fugitive slaves, peasant rebels, and penniless bastards; he then organized an army which increased so much that he became famous and was in great demand.

He succoured in turn the Dauphin of France, the King of England, the Templars of Jerusalem, the General of the Parths, the Negus of Abyssinia and the Emperor of Calicut. He fought against Scandinavians covered with fish-scales, against negroes mounted on red asses and armed with shields made of hippopotamus hide, against gold-coloured Indians who wielded great, shining swords above their heads. He conquered the Troglodytes and the cannibals. He travelled through regions so torrid that the heat of the sun would set fire to the hair on one's head; he journeyed through countries so glacial that one's arms would fall from the body; and he passed through places where the fogs were so dense that it seemed like being surrounded by phantoms.

Republics in trouble consulted him; when he conferred with ambassadors, he always obtained unexpected concessions. Also, if a monarch behaved badly, he would arrive on the scene and rebuke him. He freed nations. He rescued queens sequestered in towers. It was he and no other that killed the serpent of Milan and the dragon of Oberbirbach.

Now, the Emperor of Occitania, having triumphed over the Spanish Mussulmans, had taken the sister of the Caliph of Cordova as a concubine, and had had one daughter by her, whom he brought up in the teachings of Christ. But the Caliph, feigning that he wished to become converted, made him a visit, and brought with him a numerous escort. He slaughtered the entire garrison and threw the Emperor into a dungeon, and treated him with great cruelty in order to obtain possession of his treasures.

Julian went to his assistance, destroyed the army of infidels, laid siege to the city, slew the Caliph, chopped off his head and threw it over the fortifications like a cannon-ball.

As a reward for so great a service, the Emperor presented him with a large sum of money in baskets; but Julian declined it. Then the Emperor, thinking that the amount was not sufficiently large, offered him three quarters of his fortune, and on meeting a second refusal, proposed to share his kingdom with his benefactor. But Julian only thanked him for it, and the Emperor felt like weeping with vexation at not being able to show his gratitude, when he suddenly tapped his forehead and whispered a few words in the ear of one of his courtiers; the tapestry curtains parted and a young girl appeared.

Her large black eyes shone like two soft lights. A charming smile parted her lips. Her curls were caught in the jewels of her half-opened bodice, and the grace of her youthful body could be divined under the transparency of her tunic.

She was small and quite plump, but her waist was slender.

Julian was absolutely dazzled, all the more since he had always led a chaste life.

So he married the Emperor's daughter, and received at the same time a castle she had inherited from her mother; and when the rejoicings were over, he departed with his bride, after many courtesies had been exchanged on both sides.

The castle was of Moorish design, in white marble, erected on a promontory and surrounded by orange-trees.

Terraces of flowers extended to the shell-strewn shores of a beautiful bay. Behind the castle spread a fan-shaped forest. The sky was always blue, and the trees were swayed in turn by the ocean-breeze and by the winds that blew from the mountains that closed the horizon.

Light entered the apartments through the incrustations of the walls. High, reed-like columns supported the ceiling of the cupolas, decorated in imitation of stalactites.

Fountains played in the spacious halls; the courts were inlaid with mosaic; there were festooned partitions and a great profusion of architectural fancies; and everywhere reigned a silence so deep that the swish of a sash or the echo of a sigh could be distinctly heard.

Julian now had renounced war. Surrounded by a peaceful people, he remained idle, receiving every day a throng of subjects who came and knelt before him and kissed his hand in Oriental fashion.

Clad in sumptuous garments, he would gaze out of the window and think of his past exploits; and wish that he might again run in the desert in pursuit of ostriches and gazelles, hide among the bamboos to watch for leopards, ride through forests filled with rhinoceroses, climb the most inaccessible peaks in order to have a better aim at the eagles, and fight the polar bears on the icebergs of the northern sea.

Sometimes, in his dreams, he fancied himself like Adam in the midst of Paradise, surrounded by all the beasts; by merely extending his arm, he was able to kill them; or else they filed past him, in pairs, by order of size, from the lions and the elephants to the ermines and the ducks, as on the day they entered Noah's Ark.

Hidden in the shadow of a cave, he aimed unerring arrows at them; then came others and still others, until he awoke, wild-eyed.

Princes, friends of his, invited him to their meets, but he always refused their invitations, because he thought that by this kind of penance he might possibly avert the threatened misfortune; it seemed to him that the fate of his parents depended on his refusal to slaughter animals. He suffered because he could not see them, and his other desire was growing well-nigh unbearable.

In order to divert his mind, his wife had dancers and jugglers come to the castle.

She went abroad with him in an open litter; at other times, stretched out on the edge of a boat, they watched for hours the fish disport themselves in the water, which was as clear as the sky. Often she playfully threw flowers at him or nestling at his feet, she played melodies on an old mandolin; then, clasping her hands on his shoulder, she would inquire tremulously: "What troubles thee, my dear lord?"

He would not reply, or else he would burst into tears; but at last, one day, he confessed his fearful dread.

His wife scorned the idea and reasoned wisely with him: probably his father and mother were dead; and even if he should ever see them again, through what chance, to what end, would he arrive at this abomination? Therefore, his fears were groundless, and he should hunt again.

Julian listened to her and smiled, but he could not bring himself to yield to his desire.

One August evening when they were in their bed-chamber, she having just retired and he being about to kneel in prayer, he heard the yelping of a fox and light footsteps under the window; and he thought he saw things in the dark that looked like animals. The temptation was too strong. He seized his quiver.

His wife appeared astonished.

"I am obeying you," quoth he, "and I shall be back at sunrise."

However, she feared that some calamity would happen. But he reassured her and departed, surprised at her illogical moods.

A short time afterwards, a page came to announce that two strangers desired, in the absence of the lord of the castle, to see its mistress at once.

Soon a stooping old man and an aged woman entered the room; their coarse garments were covered with dust and each leaned on a stick.

They grew bold enough to say that they brought Julian news of his parents. She leaned out of the bed to listen to them. But after glancing at each other, the old people asked her whether he ever referred to them and if he still loved them.

"Oh! yes!" she said.

Then they exclaimed:

"We are his parents!" and they sat themselves down, for they were very tired.

But there was nothing to show the young wife that her husband was their son.

They proved it by describing to her the birthmarks he had on his body. Then she jumped out of bed, called a page, and ordered that a repast be served to them.

But although they were very hungry, they could scarcely eat, and she observed surreptitiously how their lean fingers trembled whenever they lifted their cups.

They asked a hundred questions about their son, and she answered each one of them, but she was careful not to refer to the terrible idea that concerned them.

When he failed to return, they had left their château; and had wandered for several years, following vague indications but without losing hope.

So much money had been spent at the tolls of the rivers and in inns, to satisfy the rights of princes and the demands of highwaymen, that now their purse was quite empty and they were obliged to beg. But what did it matter, since they were about to clasp again their son in their arms? They lauded his happiness in having such a beautiful wife, and did not tire of looking at her and kissing her.

The luxuriousness of the apartment astonished them; and the old man, after examining the walls, inquired why they bore the coat-of-arms of the Emperor of Occitania.

"He is my father," she replied.

And he marvelled and remembered the prediction of the gipsy, while his wife meditated upon the words the hermit had spoken to her. The glory of their son was undoubtedly only the dawn of eternal splendours, and the old people remained awed while the light from the candelabra on the table fell on them.

In the heyday of youth, both had been extremely handsome. The mother had not lost her hair, and bands of snowy whiteness framed her cheeks; and the father, with his stalwart figure and long beard, looked like a carved image.

Julian's wife prevailed upon them not to wait for him. She put them in her bed and closed the curtains; and they both fell asleep. The day broke and outdoors the little birds began to chirp.

Meanwhile, Julian had left the castle grounds and walked nervously through the forest, enjoying the velvety softness of the grass and the balminess of the air.

The shadow of the trees fell on the earth. Here and there, the moonlight flecked the glades and Julian feared to advance, because he mistook the silvery light for water and the tranquil surface of the pools for grass. A great stillness reigned everywhere, and he failed to see any of the beasts that only a moment ago were prowling around the castle. As he walked on, the woods grew thicker, and the darkness more impenetrable. Warm winds, filled with enervating perfumes, caressed him; he sank into masses of dead leaves, and after a while he leaned against an oak-tree to rest and catch his breath.

Suddenly a body blacker than the surrounding darkness sprang from behind the tree. It was a wild boar. Julian did not have time to stretch his bow, and he bewailed the fact as if it were some great misfortune. Presently, having left the woods, he beheld a wolf slinking along a hedge.

He aimed an arrow at him. The wolf paused, turned his head and quietly continued on his way. He trotted along, always keeping at the same distance, pausing now and then to look around and resuming his flight as soon as an arrow was aimed in his direction.

In this way Julian traversed an apparently endless plain, then sand-hills, and at last found himself on a plateau, that dominated a great stretch of land. Large flat stones were interspersed among crumbling vaults; bones and skeletons covered the ground, and here and there some mouldy crosses stood desolate. But presently, shapes moved in the darkness of the tombs, and from them came panting, wild-eyed hyenas. They approached him and smelled him, grinning hideously and disclosing their gums. He whipped out his sword, but they scattered in every direction and continuing their swift, limping gallop, disappeared in a cloud of dust.

Some time afterwards, in a ravine, he encountered a wild bull, with threatening horns, pawing the sand with his hoofs. Julian thrust his lance between his dewlaps. But his weapon snapped as if the beast were made of bronze; then he closed his eyes in anticipation of his death. When he opened them again, the bull had vanished.

Then his soul collapsed with shame. Some supernatural power destroyed his strength, and he set out for home through the forest. The woods were a tangle of creeping plants that he had to cut with his sword, and while he was thus engaged, a weasel slid between his feet, a panther jumped over his shoulder, and a serpent wound itself around the ash-tree.

Among its leaves was a monstrous jackdaw that watched Julian intently, and here and there, between the branches, appeared great, fiery sparks as if the sky were raining all its stars upon the forest. But the sparks were the eyes of wild-cats, owls, squirrels, monkeys and parrots.

Julian aimed his arrows at them, but the feathered weapons lighted on the leaves of the trees and looked like white butterflies. He threw stones at them; but the missiles did not strike, and fell to the ground. Then he cursed himself, and howled imprecations, and in his rage he could have struck himself.

Then all the beasts he had pursued appeared, and formed a narrow circle around him. Some sat on their hindquarters, while others stood at full height. And Julian remained among them, transfixed with terror and absolutely unable to move. By a supreme effort of his will-power, he took a step forward; those that perched in the trees opened their wings, those that trod the earth moved their limbs, and all accompanied him.

The hyenas strode in front of him, the wolf and the wild boar brought up the rear. On his right, the bull swung its head and on his left the serpent crawled through the grass; while the panther, arching its back, advanced with velvety footfalls and long strides. Julian walked as slowly as possible, so as not to irritate them, while in the depth of bushes he could distinguish porcupines, foxes, vipers, jackals, and bears.

He began to run; the brutes followed him. The serpent hissed, the malodorous beasts frothed at the mouth, the wild boar rubbed his tusks against his heels, and the wolf scratched the palms of his hands with the hairs of his snout. The monkeys pinched him and made faces, the weasel tolled over his feet. A bear knocked his cap off with its huge paw, and the panther disdainfully dropped an arrow it was about to put in its mouth.

Irony seemed to incite their sly actions. As they watched him out of the corners of their eyes, they seemed to meditate a plan of revenge, and Julian, who was deafened by the buzzing of the insects, bruised by the wings and tails of the birds, choked by the stench of animal breaths, walked with outstretched arms and closed lids, like a blind man, without even the strength to beg for mercy.

The crowing of a cock vibrated in the air. Other cocks responded; it was day; and Julian recognised the top of his palace rising above the orange-trees.

Then, on the edge of a field, he beheld some red partridges fluttering around a stubble-field. He unfastened his cloak and threw it over them like a net. When he lifted it, he found only a bird that had been dead a long time and was decaying.

This disappointment irritated him more than all the others. The thirst for carnage stirred afresh within him; animals failing him, he desired to slaughter men.

He climbed the three terraces and opened the door with a blow of his fist; but at the foot of the staircase, the memory of his beloved wife softened his heart. No doubt she was asleep, and he would go up and surprise her. Having removed his sandals, he unlocked the door softly and entered.

The stained windows dimmed the pale light of dawn. Julian stumbled over some garment's lying on the floor and a little further on, he knocked against a table covered with dishes. "She must have eaten," he thought; so he advanced cautiously towards the bed which was concealed by the darkness in the back of the room. When he reached the edge, he leaned over the pillow where the two heads were resting close together and stooped to kiss his wife. His mouth encountered a man's beard.

He fell back, thinking he had become crazed; then he approached the bed again and his searching fingers discovered some hair which seemed to be very long. In order to convince himself that he was mistaken, he once more passed his hand slowly over the pillow. But this time he was sure that it was a beard and that a man was there! a man lying beside his wife!

Flying into an ungovernable passion, he sprang upon them with his drawn dagger, foaming, stamping and howling like a wild beast. After a while he stopped.

The corpses, pierced through the heart, had not even moved. He listened attentively to the two death-rattles, they were almost alike, and as they grew fainter, another voice, coming from far away, seemed to continue them. Uncertain at first, this plaintive voice came nearer and nearer, grew louder and louder and presently he recognised, with a feeling of abject terror, the bellowing of the great black stag.

And as he turned around, he thought he saw the spectre of his wife standing at the threshold with a light in her hand.

The sound of the murder had aroused her. In one glance she understood what had happened and fled in horror, letting the candle drop from her hand. Julian picked it up.

His father and mother lay before him, stretched on their backs, with gaping wounds in their breasts; and their faces, the expression of which was full of tender dignity, seemed to hide what might be an eternal secret.

Splashes and blotches of blood were on their white skin, on the bed-clothes, on the floor, and on an ivory Christ which hung in the alcove.

The scarlet reflection of the stained window, which just then was struck by the sun, lighted up the bloody spots and appeared to scatter them around the whole room. Julian walked toward the corpses, repeating to himself and trying to believe that he was mistaken, that it was not possible, that there are often inexplicable likenesses.

At last he bent over to look closely at the old man and he saw, between the half-closed lids, a dead pupil that scorched him like fire. Then he went over to the other side of the bed, where the other corpse lay, but the face was partly hidden by bands of white hair. Julian slipped his finger beneath them and raised the head, holding it at arm's length to study its features, while, with his other hand he lifted the torch. Drops of blood oozed from the mattress and fell one by one upon the floor.

At the close of the day, he appeared before his wife, and in a changed voice commanded her first not to answer him, not to approach him, not even to look at him, and to obey, under the penalty of eternal damnation, every one of his orders, which were irrevocable.

The funeral was to be held in accordance with the written instructions he had left on a chair in the death-chamber.

He left her his castle, his vassals, all his worldly goods, without keeping even his clothes or his sandals, which would be found at the top of the stairs.

She had obeyed the will of God in bringing about his crime, and accordingly she must pray for his soul, since henceforth he should cease to exist.

The dead were buried sumptuously in the chapel of a monastery which it took three days to reach from the castle. A monk wearing a hood that covered his head followed the procession alone, for nobody dared to speak to him. And during the mass, he lay flat on the floor with his face downward and his arms stretched out at his sides.

After the burial, he was seen to take the road leading into the mountains. He looked back several times, and finally passed out of sight.

III

The Reparation

He left the country and begged his daily bread on his way.

He stretched out his hand to the horsemen he met in the roads, and humbly approached the harvesters in the fields; or else remained motionless in front of the gates of castles; and his face was so sad that he was never turned away.

Obeying a spirit of humility, he related his history to all men, and they would flee from him and cross themselves. In villages through which he had passed before, the good people bolted the doors, threatened him, and threw stones at him as soon as they recognised him. The more charitable ones placed a bowl on the window-sill and closed the shutters in order to avoid seeing him.

Repelled and shunned by everyone, he avoided his fellow-men and nourished himself with roots and plants, stray fruits and shells which he gathered along the shores.

Often, at the bend of a hill, he could perceive a mass of crowded roofs, stone spires, bridges, towers and narrow streets, from which arose a continual murmur of activity.

The desire to mingle with men impelled him to enter the city. But the gross and beastly expression of their faces, the noise of their industries and the indifference of their remarks, chilled his very heart. On holidays, when the cathedral bells rang out at daybreak and filled the people's hearts with gladness, he watched the inhabitants coming out of their dwellings, the dancers in the public squares, the fountains of ale, the damask hangings spread before the houses of princes; and then, when night came, he would peer through the windows at the long tables where families gathered and where grandparents held little children on their knees; then sobs would rise in his throat and he would turn away and go back to his haunts.

He gazed with yearning at the colts in the pastures, the birds in their nests, the insects on the flowers; but they all fled from him at his approach and hid or flew away. So he sought solitude. But the wind brought to his ears sounds resembling death-rattles; the tears of the dew reminded him of heavier drops, and every evening, the sun would spread blood in the sky, and every night, in his dreams, he lived over his parricide.

He made himself a hair-cloth lined with iron spikes. On his knees, he ascended every hill that was crowned with a chapel. But the unrelenting thought spoiled the splendour of the tabernacles and tortured him in the midst of his penances.

He did not rebel against God, who had inflicted his action, but he despaired at the thought that he had committed it.

He had such a horror of himself that he took all sorts of risks. He rescued paralytics from fire and children from waves. But the ocean scorned him and the flames spared him. Time did not allay his torment, which became so intolerable that he resolved to die.

One day, while he was stooping over a fountain to judge of its depth, an old man appeared on the other side. He wore a white beard and his appearance was so lamentable that Julian could not keep back his tears. The old man also was weeping. Without recognising him, Julian remembered confusedly a face that resembled his. He uttered a cry; for it was his father who stood before him; and he gave up all thought of taking his own life.

Thus weighted down by his recollections, he travelled through many countries and arrived at a river which was dangerous, because of its violence and the slime that covered its shores. Since a long time nobody had ventured to cross it.

The bow of an old boat, whose stern was buried in the mud, showed among the reeds. Julian, on examining it closely, found a pair of oars and hit upon the idea of devoting his life to the service of his fellow-men.

He began by establishing on the bank of the river a sort of road which would enable people to approach the edge of the stream; he broke his nails in his efforts to lift enormous stones which he pressed against the pit of his stomach in order to transport them from one point to another; he slipped in the mud, he sank into it, and several times was on the very brink of death.

Then he took to repairing the boat with debris of vessels, and afterwards built himself a hut with putty and trunks of trees.

When it became known that a ferry had been established, passengers flocked to it. They hailed him from the opposite side by waving flags, and Julian would jump into the boat and row over. The craft was very heavy, and the people loaded it with all sorts of baggage, and beasts of burden, who reared with fright, thereby adding greatly to the confusion. He asked nothing for his trouble; some gave him left-over victuals which they took from their sacks or worn-out garments which they could no longer use.

The brutal ones hurled curses at him, and when he rebuked them gently they replied with insults, and he was content to bless them.

A little table, a stool, a bed made of dead leaves and three earthen bowls were all he possessed. Two holes in the wall served as windows. On one side, as far as the eye could see, stretched barren wastes studded here and there with pools of water; and in front of him flowed the greenish waters of the wide river. In the spring, a putrid odour arose from the damp sod. Then fierce gales lifted clouds of dust that blew everywhere, even settling in the water and in one's mouth. A little later swarms of mosquitoes appeared, whose buzzing and stinging continued night and day. After that, came frightful frosts which communicated a stone-like rigidity to everything and inspired one with an insane desire for meat. Months passed when Julian never saw a human being. He often closed his lids and endeavored to recall his youth;—he beheld the courtyard of a castle, with greyhounds stretched out on a terrace, an armoury filled with valets, and under a bower of vines a youth with blond curls, sitting between an old man wrapped in furs and a lady with a high cap; presently the corpses rose before him, and then he would throw himself face downward on his cot and sob:

"Oh! poor father! poor mother! poor mother!" and would drop into a fitful slumber in which the terrible visions recurred.

One night he thought that some one was calling to him in his sleep. He listened intently, but could hear nothing save the roaring of the waters.

But the same voice repeated: "Julian!"

It proceeded from the opposite shore, fact which appeared extraordinary to him, considering the breadth of the river.

The voice called a third time: "Julian!"

And the high-pitched tones sounded like the ringing of a church-bell.

Having lighted his lantern, he stepped out of his cabin. A frightful storm raged. The darkness was complete and was illuminated here and there only by the white waves leaping and tumbling.

After a moment's hesitation, he untied the rope. The water presently grew smooth and the boat glided easily to the opposite shore, where a man was waiting.

He was wrapped in a torn piece of linen; his face was like a chalk mask, and his eyes were redder than glowing coals. When Julian held up his lantern he noticed that the stranger was covered with hideous sores; but notwithstanding this, there was in his attitude something like the majesty of a king.

As soon as he stepped into the boat, it sank deep into the water, borne downward by his weight; then it rose again and Julian began to row.

With each stroke of the oars, the force of the waves raised the bow of the boat. The water, which was blacker than ink, ran furiously along the sides. It formed abysses and then mountains, over which the boat glided, then it fell into yawning depths where, buffeted by the wind, it whirled around and around.

Julian leaned far forward and, bracing himself with his feet, bent backwards so as to bring his whole strength into play. Hail-stones cut his hands, the rain ran down his back, the velocity of the wind suffocated him. He stopped rowing and let the boat drift with the tide. But realising that an important matter was at stake, a command which could not be disregarded, he picked up the oars again; and the rattling of the tholes mingled with the clamourings of the storm.

The little lantern burned in front of him. Sometimes birds fluttered past it and obscured the light. But he could distinguish the eyes of the leper who stood at the stern, as motionless as a column.

And the trip lasted a long, long time.

When they reached the hut, Julian closed the door and saw the man sit down on the stool. The species of shroud that was wrapped around him had fallen below his loins, and his shoulders and chest and lean arms were hidden under blotches of scaly pustules. Enormous wrinkles crossed his forehead. Like a skeleton, he had a hole instead of a nose, and from his bluish lips came breath which was fetid and as thick as mist.

"I am hungry," he said.

Julian set before him what he had, a piece of pork and some crusts of coarse bread.

After he had devoured them, the table, the bowl, and the handle of the knife bore the same scales that covered his body.

Then he said: "I thirst!"

Julian fetched his jug of water and when he lifted it, he smelled an aroma that dilated his nostrils and filled his heart with gladness. It was wine; what a boon! but the leper stretched out his arm and emptied the jug at one draught.

Then he said: "I am cold!"

Julian ignited a bundle of ferns that lay in the middle of the hut. The leper approached the fire and, resting on his heels, began to warm himself; his whole frame shook and he was failing visibly; his eyes grew dull, his sores began to break, and in a faint voice he whispered:

"Thy bed!"

Julian helped him gently to it, and even laid the sail of his boat over him to keep him warm.

The leper tossed and moaned. The corners of his mouth were drawn up over his teeth; an accelerated death-rattle shook his chest and with each one of his aspirations, his stomach touched his spine. At last, he closed his eyes.

"I feel as if ice were in my bones! Lay thyself beside me!" he commanded. Julian took off his garments; and then, as naked as on the day he was born, he got into the bed; against his thigh he could feel the skin of the leper, and it was colder than a serpent and as rough as a file.

He tried to encourage the leper, but he only whispered:

"Oh! I am about to die! Come closer to me and warm me! Not with thy hands! No! with thy whole body."

So Julian stretched himself out upon the leper, lay on him, lips to lips, chest to chest.

Then the leper clasped him close and presently his eyes shone like stars; his hair lengthened into sunbeams; the breath of his nostrils had the scent of roses; a cloud of incense rose from the hearth, and the waters began to murmur harmoniously; an abundance of bliss, a superhuman joy, filled the soul of the swooning Julian, while he who clasped him to his breast grew and grew until his head and his feet touched the opposite walls of the cabin. The roof flew up in the air, disclosing the heavens, and Julian ascended into infinity face to face with our Lord Jesus Christ, who bore him straight to heaven.

And this is the story of Saint Julian the Hospitaller, as it is given on the stained-glass window of a church in my birthplace.

A SIMPLE SOUL

I

Félicité

For half a century the housewives of Pont-l'Evêque had envied Madame Aubain her servant Félicité.

For a hundred francs a year, she cooked and did the housework, washed, ironed, mended, harnessed the horse, fattened the poultry, made the butter and remained faithful to her mistress—although the latter was by no means an agreeable person.

Madame Aubain had married a comely youth without any money, who died in the beginning of 1809, leaving her with two young children and a number of debts. She sold all her property excepting the farm of Toucques and the farm of Geffosses, the income of which barely amounted to 5,000 francs; then she left her house in Saint-Melaine, and moved into a less pretentious one which had belonged to her ancestors and stood back of the market-place. This house, with its slate-covered roof, was built between a passage-way and a narrow street that led to the river. The interior was so unevenly graded that it caused people to stumble. A narrow hall separated the kitchen from the parlour, where Madame Aubain sat all day in a straw armchair near the window. Eight mahogany chairs stood in a row against the white wainscoting. An old piano, standing beneath a barometer, was covered with a pyramid of old books and boxes. On either side of the yellow marble mantelpiece, in Louis XV style, stood a tapestry armchair. The clock represented a temple of Vesta; and the whole room smelled musty, as it was on a lower level than the garden.

On the first floor was Madame's bedchamber, a large room papered in a flowered design and containing the portrait of Monsieur dressed in the costume of a dandy. It communicated with a smaller room, in which there were two little cribs, without any mattresses. Next, came the parlour (always closed), filled with furniture covered with sheets. Then a hall, which led to the study, where books and papers were piled on the shelves of a book-case that enclosed three quarters of the big black desk. Two panels were entirely hidden under pen-and-ink sketches, Gouache landscapes and Audran engravings, relics of better times and vanished luxury. On the second floor, a garret-window lighted Félicité's room, which looked out upon the meadows.

She arose at daybreak, in order to attend mass, and she worked without interruption until night; then, when dinner was over, the dishes cleared away and the door securely locked, she would bury the log under the ashes and fall asleep in front of the hearth with a rosary in her hand. Nobody could bargain with greater obstinacy, and as for cleanliness, the lustre on her brass saucepans was the envy and despair of other servants. She was most economical, and when she ate she would gather up crumbs with the tip of her finger, so that nothing should be wasted of the loaf of bread weighing twelve pounds which was baked especially for her and lasted three weeks.

Summer and winter she wore a dimity kerchief fastened in the back with a pin, a cap which concealed her hair, a red skirt, grey stockings, and an apron with a bib like those worn by hospital nurses.

Her face was thin and her voice shrill. When she was twenty-five, she looked forty. After she had passed fifty, nobody could tell her age; erect and silent always, she resembled a wooden figure working automatically.

II

The Heroine

Like every other woman, she had had an affair of the heart. Her father, who was a mason, was killed by falling from a scaffolding. Then her mother died and her sisters went their different ways; a farmer took her in, and while she was quite small, let her keep cows in the fields. She was clad in miserable rags, beaten for the slightest offence and finally dismissed for a theft of thirty sous which she did not commit. She took service on another farm where she tended the poultry; and as she was well thought of by her master, her fellow-workers soon grew jealous.

One evening in August (she was then eighteen years old), they persuaded her to accompany them to the fair at Colleville. She was immediately dazzled by the noise, the lights in the trees, the brightness of the dresses, the laces and gold crosses, and the crowd of people all hopping at the same time. She was standing modestly at a distance, when presently a young man of well-to-do appearance, who had been leaning on the pole of a wagon and smoking his pipe, approached her, and asked her for a dance. He treated her to cider and cake, bought her a silk shawl, and then, thinking she had guessed his purpose, offered to see her home. When they came to the end of a field he threw her down brutally. But she grew frightened and screamed, and he walked off.

One evening, on the road leading to Beaumont, she came upon a wagon loaded with hay, and when she overtook it, she recognised Théodore. He greeted her calmly, and asked her to forget what had happened between them, as it "was all the fault of the drink."

She did not know what to reply and wished to run away.

Presently he began to speak of the harvest and of the notables of the village; his father had left Colleville and bought the farm of Les Écots, so that now they would be neighbors. "Ah!" she exclaimed. He then added that his parents were looking around for a wife for him, but that he, himself, was not so anxious and preferred to wait for a girl who suited him. She hung her head. He then asked her whether she had ever thought of marrying. She replied, smilingly, that it was wrong of him to make fun of her. "Oh! no, I am in earnest," he said, and put his left arm around her waist while they sauntered along. The air was soft, the stars were bright, and the huge load of hay oscillated in front of them, drawn by four horses whose ponderous hoofs raised clouds of dust. Without a word from their driver they turned to the right. He kissed her again and she went home. The following week, Théodore obtained meetings.

They met in yards, behind walls or under isolated trees. She was not ignorant, as girls of well-to-do families are—for the animals had instructed her;—but her reason and her instinct of honour kept her from falling. Her resistance exasperated Théodore's love and so in order to satisfy it (or perchance ingenuously), he offered to marry her. She would not believe him at first, so he made solemn promises. But, in a short time he mentioned a difficulty; the previous year, his parents had purchased a substitute for him; but any day he might be drafted and the prospect of serving in the army alarmed him greatly. To Félicité his cowardice appeared a proof of his love for her, and her devotion to him grew stronger. When she met him, he would torture her with his fears and his entreaties. At last, he announced that he was going to the prefect himself for information, and would let her know everything on the following Sunday, between eleven o'clock and midnight.

When the time drew near, she ran to meet her lover.

But instead of Théodore, one of his friends was at the meeting-place.

He informed her that she would never see her sweetheart again; for, in order to escape the conscription, he had married a rich old woman, Madame Lehoussais, of Toucques.

The poor girl's sorrow was frightful. She threw herself on the ground, she cried and called on the Lord, and wandered around desolately until sunrise. Then she went back to the farm, declared her intention of leaving, and at the end of the month, after she had received her wages, she packed all her belongings in a handkerchief and started for Pont-l'Evêque.

In front of the inn, she met a woman wearing widow's weeds, and upon questioning her, learned that she was looking for a cook. The girl did not know very much, but appeared so willing and so modest in her requirements, that Madame Aubain finally said:

"Very well, I will give you a trial."

And half an hour later Félicité was installed in her house.

At first she lived in a constant anxiety that was caused by "the style of the household" and the memory of "Monsieur," that hovered over everything. Paul and Virginia, the one aged seven, and the other barely four, seemed made of some precious material; she carried them pig-a-back, and was greatly mortified when Madame Aubain forbade her to kiss them every other minute.

But in spite of all this, she was happy. The comfort of her new surroundings had obliterated her sadness.

Every Thursday, friends of Madame Aubain dropped in for a game of cards, and it was Félicité's duty to prepare the table and heat the foot-warmers. They arrived at exactly eight o'clock and departed before eleven.

Every Monday morning, the dealer in second-hand goods, who lived under the alley-way, spread out his wares on the sidewalk. Then the city would be filled with a buzzing of voices in which the neighing of horses, the bleating of lambs, the grunting of pigs, could be distinguished, mingled with the sharp sound of wheels on the cobble-stones. About twelve o'clock, when the market was in full swing, there appeared at the front door a tall, middle-aged peasant, with a hooked nose and a cap on the back of his head; it was Robelin, the farmer of Geffosses. Shortly afterwards came Liébard, the farmer of Toucques, short, rotund and ruddy, wearing a grey jacket and spurred boots.

Both men brought their landlady either chickens or cheese. Félicité would invariably thwart their ruses and they held her in great respect.

At various times, Madame Aubain received a visit from the Marquis de Grémanville, one of her uncles, who was ruined and lived at Falaise on the remainder of his estates. He always came at dinner-time and brought an ugly poodle with him, whose paws soiled the furniture. In spite of his efforts to appear a man of breeding (he even went so far as to raise his hat every time he said "My deceased father"), his habits got the better of him, and he would fill his glass a little too often and relate broad stories. Félicité would show him out very politely and say: "You have had enough for this time, Monsieur de Grémanville! Hoping to see you again!" and would close the door.

She opened it gladly for Monsieur Bourais, a retired lawyer. His bald head and white cravat, the ruffling of his shirt, his flowing brown coat, the manner in which he took his snuff, his whole person, in fact, produced in her the kind of awe which we feel when we see extraordinary persons. As he managed Madame's estates, he spent hours with her in Monsieur's study; he was in constant fear of being compromised, had a great regard for the magistracy and some pretensions to learning.

In order to facilitate the children's studies, he presented them with an engraved geography which represented various scenes of the world: cannibals with feather head-dresses, a gorilla kidnapping a young girl, Arabs in the desert, a whale being harpooned, etc.

Paul explained the pictures to Félicité. And, in fact, this was her only literary education.

The children's studies were under the direction of a poor devil employed at the town-hall, who sharpened his pocketknife on his boots and was famous for his penmanship.

When the weather was fine, they went to Geffosses. The house was built in the centre of the sloping yard; and the sea looked like a grey spot in the distance. Félicité would take slices of cold meat from the lunch basket and they would sit down and eat in a room next to the dairy. This room was all that remained of a cottage that had been torn down. The dilapidated wall-paper trembled in the drafts. Madame Aubain, overwhelmed by recollections, would hang her head, while the children were afraid to open their mouths. Then, "Why don't you go and play?" their mother would say; and they would scamper off.

Paul would go to the old barn, catch birds, throw stones into the pond, or pound the trunks of the trees with a stick till they resounded like drums. Virginia would feed the rabbits and run to pick the wild flowers in the fields, and her flying legs would disclose her little embroidered pantalettes. One autumn evening, they struck out for home through the meadows. The new moon illumined part of the sky and a mist hovered like a veil over the sinuosities of the river. Oxen, lying in the pastures, gazed mildly at the passing persons. In the third field, however, several of them got up and surrounded them. "Don't be afraid," cried Félicité; and murmuring a sort of lament she passed her hand over the back of the nearest ox; he turned away and the others followed. But when they came to the next pasture, they heard frightful bellowing.

It was a bull which was hidden from them by the fog. He advanced towards the two women, and Madame Aubain prepared to flee for her life. "No, no! not so fast," warned Félicité. Still they hurried on, for they could hear the noisy breathing of the bull close behind them. His hoofs pounded the grass like hammers, and presently he began to gallop! Félicité turned around and threw patches of grass in his eyes. He hung his head, shook his horns and bellowed with fury. Madame Aubain and the children, huddled at the end of the field, were trying to jump over the ditch. Félicité continued to back before the bull, blinding him with dirt, while she shouted to them to make haste.

Madame Aubain finally slid into the ditch, after shoving first Virginia and then Paul into it, and though she stumbled several times she managed, by dint of courage, to climb the other side of it.

The bull had driven Félicité up against a fence; the foam from his muzzle flew in her face and in another minute he would have disembowelled her. She had just time to slip between two bars and the huge animal, thwarted, paused.

For years, this occurrence was a topic of conversation in Pont-l'Evêque. But Félicité took no credit to herself, and probably never knew that she had been heroic.

Virginia occupied her thoughts solely, for the shock she had sustained gave her a nervous affection, and the physician, M. Poupart, prescribed the saltwater bathing at Trouville. In those days, Trouville was not greatly patronised. Madame Aubain gathered information, consulted Bourais, and made preparations as if they were going on an extended trip.

The baggage was sent the day before on Liébard's cart. On the following morning, he brought around two horses, one of which had a woman's saddle with a velveteen back to it, while on the crupper of the other was a rolled shawl that was to be used for a seat. Madame Aubain mounted the second horse, behind Liébard. Félicité took charge of the little girl, and Paul rode M. Lechaptois' donkey, which had been lent for the occasion on the condition that they should be careful of it.

The road was so bad that it took two hours to cover the eight miles. The two horses sank knee-deep into the mud and stumbled into ditches; sometimes they had to jump over them. In certain places, Liébard's mare stopped abruptly. He waited patiently till she started again, and talked of the people whose estates bordered the road, adding his own moral reflections to the outline of their histories. Thus, when they were passing through Toucques, and came to some windows draped with nasturtiums, he shrugged his shoulders and said: "There's a woman, Madame Lehoussais, who, instead of taking a young man—" Félicité could not catch what followed; the horses began to trot, the donkey to gallop, and they turned into a lane; then a gate swung open, two farm-hands appeared and they all dismounted at the very threshold of the farm-house.

Mother Liébard, when she caught sight of her mistress, was lavish with joyful demonstrations. She got up a lunch which comprised a leg of mutton, tripe, sausages, a chicken fricassée, sweet cider, a fruit tart and some preserved prunes; then to all this the good woman added polite remarks about Madame, who appeared to be in better health, Mademoiselle, who had grown to be "superb," and Paul, who had become singularly sturdy; she spoke also of their deceased grandparents, whom the Liébards had known, for they had been in the service of the family for several generations.

Like its owners, the farm had an ancient appearance. The beams of the ceiling were mouldy, the walls black with smoke and the windows grey with dust. The oak sideboard was filled with all sorts of utensils, plates, pitchers, tin bowls, wolf-traps. The children laughed when they saw a huge syringe. There was not a tree in the yard that did not have mushrooms growing around its foot, or a bunch of mistletoe hanging in its branches. Several of the trees had been blown down, but they had started to grow in the middle and all were laden with quantities of apples. The thatched roofs, which were of unequal thickness, looked like brown velvet and could resist the fiercest gales. But the wagon-shed was fast crumbling to ruins. Madame Aubain said that she would attend to it, and then gave orders to have the horses saddled.

It took another thirty minutes to reach Trouville. The little caravan dismounted in order to pass Les Écores, a cliff that overhangs the bay, and a few minutes later, at the end of the dock, they entered the yard of the Golden Lamb, an inn kept by Mother David.

During the first few days, Virginia felt stronger, owing to the change of air and the action of the sea-baths. She took them in her little chemise, as she had no bathing suit, and afterwards her nurse dressed her in the cabin of a customs officer, which was used for that purpose by other bathers.

In the afternoon, they would take the donkey and go to the Roches-Noires, near Hennequeville. The path led at first through undulating grounds, and thence to a plateau, where pastures and tilled fields alternated. At the edge of the road, mingling with the brambles, grew holly bushes, and here and there stood large dead trees whose branches traced zigzags upon the blue sky.

Ordinarily, they rested in a field facing the ocean, with Deauville on their left, and Havre on their right. The sea glittered brightly in the sun and was as smooth as a mirror, and so calm that they could scarcely distinguish its murmur; sparrows chirped joyfully and the immense canopy of heaven spread over it all. Madame Aubain brought out her sewing, and Virginia amused herself by braiding reeds; Félicité wove lavender blossoms, while Paul was bored and wished to go home.

Sometimes they crossed the Toucques in a boat, and started to hunt for seashells. The outgoing tide exposed starfish and sea-urchins, and the children tried to catch the flakes of foam which the wind blew away. The sleepy waves lapping the sand unfurled themselves along the shore that extended as far as the eye could see, but where land began, it was limited by the downs which separated it from the "Swamp," a large meadow shaped like a hippodrome. When they went home that way, Trouville, on the slope of a hill below, grew larger and larger as they advanced, and, with all its houses of unequal height, seemed to spread out before them in a sort of giddy confusion.

When the heat was too oppressive, they remained in their rooms. The dazzling sunlight cast bars of light between the shutters. Not a sound in the village, not a soul on the sidewalk. This silence intensified the tranquillity of everything. In the distance, the hammers of some calkers pounded the hull of a ship, and the sultry breeze brought them an odour of tar.

The principal diversion consisted in watching the return of the fishing-smacks. As soon as they passed the beacons, they began to ply to windward. The sails were lowered to one third of the masts, and with their foresails swelled up like balloons they glided over the waves and anchored in the middle of the harbour. Then they crept up alongside of the dock and the sailors threw the quivering fish over the side of the boat; a line of carts was waiting for them, and women with white caps sprang forward to receive the baskets and embrace their men-folk.

One day, one of them spoke to Félicité, who, after a little while, returned to the house gleefully. She had found one of her sisters, and presently Nastasie Barette, wife of Léroux, made her appearance, holding an infant in her arms, another child by the hand, while on her left was a little cabin-boy with his hands in his pockets and his cap on his ear.

At the end of fifteen minutes, Madame Aubain bade her go.

They always hung around the kitchen, or approached Félicité when she and the children were out walking. The husband, however, did not show himself.

Félicité developed a great fondness for them; she bought them a stove, some shirts and a blanket; it was evident that they exploited her. Her foolishness annoyed Madame Aubain, who, moreover did not like the nephew's familiarity, for he called her son "thou";—and, as Virginia began to cough and the season was over, she decided to return to Pont-l'Evêque.

Monsieur Bourais assisted her in the choice of a college. The one at Caën was considered the best. So Paul was sent away and bravely said good-bye to them all, for he was glad to go to live in a house where he would have boy companions.

Madame Aubain resigned herself to the separation from her son because it was unavoidable. Virginia brooded less and less over it. Félicité regretted the noise he made, but soon a new occupation diverted her mind; beginning from Christmas, she accompanied the little girl to her catechism lesson every day.

III

Death

After she had made a curtsey at the threshold, she would walk up the aisle between the double lines of chairs, open Madame Aubain's pew, sit down and look around.

Girls and boys, the former on the right, the latter on the left-hand side of the church, filled the stalls of the choir; the priest stood beside the reading-desk; on one stained window of the side-aisle the Holy Ghost hovered over the Virgin; on another one, Mary knelt before the Child Jesus, and behind the altar, a wooden group represented Saint Michael felling the dragon.

The priest first read a condensed lesson of sacred history. Félicité evoked Paradise, the Flood, the Tower of Babel, the blazing cities, the dying nations, the shattered idols; and out of this she developed a great respect for the Almighty and a great fear of His wrath. Then, when she listened to the Passion, she wept. Why had they crucified Him who loved little children, nourished the people, made the blind see, and who, out of humility, had wished to be born among the poor, in a stable? The sowings, the harvests, the wine-presses, all those familiar things which the Scriptures mention, formed a part of her life; the word of God sanctified them; and she loved the lambs with increased tenderness for the sake of the Lamb, and the doves because of the Holy Ghost.

She found it hard, however, to think of the latter as a person, for was it not a bird, a flame, and sometimes only a breath? Perhaps it is its light that at night hovers over swamps, its breath that propels the clouds, its voice that renders church-bells harmonious. And Félicité worshipped devoutly, while enjoying the coolness and the stillness of the church.

As for the dogma, she could not understand it and did not even try. The priest discoursed, the children recited, and she went to sleep, only to awaken with a start when they were leaving the church and their wooden shoes clattered on the stone pavement.

In this way, she learned her catechism, her religious education having been neglected in her youth; and thenceforth she imitated all Virginia's religious practises, fasted when she did, and went to confession with her. At the Corpus-Christi Day they both decorated an altar.

She worried in advance over Virginia's first communion. She fussed about the shoes, the rosary, the book and the gloves. With what nervousness she helped the mother dress the child!

During the entire ceremony, she felt anguished. Monsieur Bourais hid part of the choir from view, but directly in front of her, the flock of maidens, wearing white wreaths over their lowered veils, formed a snow-white field, and she recognised her darling by the slenderness of her neck and her devout attitude. The bell tinkled. All the heads bent and there was a silence. Then, at the peals of the organ the singers and the worshippers struck up the Agnus Dei; the boys' procession began; behind them came the girls. With clasped hands, they advanced step by step to the lighted altar, knelt at the first step, received one by one the Host, and returned to their seats in the same order. When Virginia's turn came, Félicité leaned forward to watch her, and through that imagination which springs from true affection, she at once became the child, whose face and dress became hers, whose heart beat in her bosom, and when Virginia opened her mouth and closed her lids, she did likewise and came very near fainting.

The following day, she presented herself early at the church so as to receive communion from the curé. She took it with the proper feeling, but did not experience the same delight as on the previous day.

Madame Aubain wished to make an accomplished girl of her daughter; and as Guyot could not teach English nor music, she decided to send her to the Ursulines at Honfleur.

The child made no objection, but Félicité sighed and thought Madame was heartless. Then, she thought that perhaps her mistress was right, as these things were beyond her sphere. Finally, one day, an old *fiacre* stopped in front of the door and a nun stepped out. Félicité put Virginia's luggage on top of the carriage, gave the coachman some instructions, and smuggled six jars of jam, a dozen pears and a bunch of violets under the seat.

At the last minute, Virginia had a fit of sobbing; she embraced her mother again and again, while the latter kissed her on her forehead, and said: "Now, be brave, be brave!" The step was pulled up and the *fiacre* rumbled off.

Then Madame Aubain had a fainting spell, and that evening all her friends, including the two Lormeaus, Madame Lechaptois, the ladies Rochefeuille, Messieurs de Houppeville and Bourais, called on her and tendered their sympathy.

At first the separation proved very painful to her. But her daughter wrote her three times a week and the other days she, herself, wrote to Virginia. Then she walked in the garden, read a little, and in this way managed to fill out the emptiness of the hours.

Each morning, out of habit, Félicité entered Virginia's room and gazed at the walls. She missed combing her hair, lacing her shoes, tucking her in her bed, and the bright face and little hand when they used to go out for a walk. In order to occupy herself she tried to make lace. But her clumsy fingers broke the threads; she had no heart for anything, lost her sleep and "wasted away," as she put it.

In order to have some distraction, she asked leave to receive the visits of her nephew Victor.

He would come on Sunday, after church, with ruddy cheeks and bared chest, bringing with him the scent of the country. She would set the table and they would sit down opposite each other, and eat their dinner; she ate as little as possible, herself, to avoid any extra expense, but would stuff him so with food that he would finally go to sleep. At the first stroke of vespers, she would wake him up, brush his trousers, tie his cravat and walk to church with him, leaning on his arm with maternal pride.

His parents always told him to get something out of her, either a package of brown sugar, or soap, or brandy, and sometimes even money. He brought her his clothes to mend, and she accepted the task gladly, because it meant another visit from him.

In August, his father took him on a coasting-vessel.

It was vacation time and the arrival of the children consoled Félicité. But Paul was capricious, and Virginia was growing too old to be thee-and-thou'd, a fact which seemed to produce a sort of embarrassment in their relations.

Victor went successively to Morlaix, to Dunkirk, and to Brighton; whenever he returned from a trip he would bring her a present. The first time it was a box of shells; the second, a coffee-cup; the third, a big doll of ginger-bread. He was growing handsome, had a good figure, a tiny moustache, kind eyes, and a little leather cap that sat jauntily on the back of his head. He amused his aunt by telling her stories mingled with nautical expressions.

One Monday, the 14th of July, 1819 (she never forgot the date), Victor announced that he had been engaged on merchant-vessel and that in two days he would take the steamer at Honfleur and join his sailer, which was going to start from Havre very soon. Perhaps he might be away two years.

The prospect of his departure filled Félicité with despair, and in order to bid him farewell, on Wednesday night, after Madame's dinner, she put on her pattens and trudged the four miles that separated Pont-l'Evêque from Honfleur.

When she reached the Calvary, instead of turning to the right, she turned to the left and lost herself in coal-yards; she had to retrace her steps; some people she spoke to advised her to hasten. She walked helplessly around the harbour filled with vessels, and knocked against hawsers. Presently the ground sloped abruptly, lights flittered to and fro, and she thought all at once that she had gone mad when she saw some horses in the sky.

Others, on the edge of the dock, neighed at the sight of the ocean. A derrick pulled them up in the air and dumped them into a boat, where passengers were bustling about among barrels of cider, baskets of cheese and bags of meal; chickens cackled, the captain swore and a cabin-boy rested on the railing, apparently indifferent to his surroundings. Félicité, who did not recognise him, kept shouting: "Victor!" He suddenly raised his eyes, but while she was preparing to rush up to him, they withdrew the gangplank.

The packet, towed by singing women, glided out of the harbour. Her hull squeaked and the heavy waves beat up against her sides. The sail had turned and nobody was visible;—and on the ocean, silvered by the light of the moon, the vessel formed a black spot that grew dimmer and dimmer, and finally disappeared.

When Félicité passed the Calvary again, she felt as if she must entrust that which was dearest to her to the Lord; and for a long while she prayed, with uplifted eyes and a face wet with tears. The city was sleeping; some customs officials were taking the air; and the water kept pouring through the holes of the dam with a deafening roar. The town clock struck two.

The parlour of the convent would not open until morning, and surely a delay would annoy Madame; so, in spite of her desire to see the other child, she went home. The maids of the inn were just arising when she reached Pont-l'Evêque.

So the poor boy would be on the ocean for months! His previous trips had not alarmed her. One can come back from England and Brittany; but America, the colonies, the islands, were all lost in an uncertain region at the very end of the world.

From that time on, Félicité thought solely of her nephew. On warm days she feared he would suffer from thirst, and when it stormed, she was afraid he would be struck by lightning. When she harkened to the wind that rattled in the chimney and dislodged the tiles on the roof, she imagined that he was being buffeted by the same storm, perched on top of a shattered mast, with his whole body bent backward and covered with sea-foam; or,—these were recollections of the engraved geography—he was being devoured by savages, or captured in a forest by apes, or dying on some lonely coast. She never mentioned her anxieties, however.

Madame Aubain worried about her daughter. The sisters thought that Virginia was affectionate but delicate. The slightest emotion enervated her. She had to give up her piano lessons. Her mother insisted upon regular letters from the convent. One morning, when the postman failed to come, she grew impatient and began to pace to and fro, from her chair to the window. It was really extraordinary! No news since four days!

In order to console her mistress by her own example, Félicité said:

"Why, Madame, I haven't had any news since six months!"—

"From whom?"—

The servant replied gently:

"Why—from my nephew."

"Oh, yes, your nephew!" And shrugging her shoulders, Madame Aubain continued to pace the floor as if to say: "I did not think of it.— Besides, I do not care, a cabin-boy, a pauper!—but my daughter—what a difference! just think of it!—"

Félicité, although she had been reared roughly, was very indignant. Then she forgot about it.

It appeared quite natural to her that one should lose one's head about Virginia.

The two children were of equal importance; they were united in her heart and their fate was to be the same.

The chemist informed her that Victor's vessel had reached Havana. He had read the information in a newspaper.

Félicité imagined that Havana was a place where people did nothing but smoke, and that Victor walked around among negroes in a cloud of tobacco. Could a person, in case of need, return by land? How far was it from Pont-l'Evêque? In order to learn these things she questioned Monsieur Bourais. He reached for his map and began some explanations concerning longitudes, and smiled with superiority at Félicité's bewilderment. At last, he took his pencil and pointed out an imperceptible black point in the scallops of an oval blotch, adding: "There it is." She bent over the map; the maze of coloured lines hurt her eyes without enlightening her; and when Bourais asked her what puzzled her, she requested him to show her the house Victor lived in. Bourais threw up his hands, sneezed, and then laughed uproariously; such ignorance delighted his soul; but Félicité failed to understand the cause of his mirth, she whose intelligence was so limited that she perhaps expected to see even the picture of her nephew!

It was two weeks later that Liébard came into the kitchen at market-time, and handed her a letter from her brother-in-law. As neither of them could read, she called upon her mistress.

Madame Aubain, who was counting the stitches of her knitting, laid her work down beside her, opened the letter, started, and in a low tone and with a searching look said: "They tell you of a—misfortune. Your nephew—."

He had died. The letter told nothing more.

Félicité dropped on a chair, leaned her head against the back and closed her lids; presently they grew pink. Then, with drooping head, inert hands and staring eyes she repeated at intervals:

"Poor little chap! poor little chap!"

Liébard watched her and sighed. Madame Aubain was trembling.

She proposed to the girl to go see her sister in Trouville.

With a single motion, Félicité replied that it was not necessary.

There was a silence. Old Liébard thought it about time for him to take leave.

Then Félicité uttered:

"They have no sympathy, they do not care!"

Her head fell forward again, and from time to time, mechanically, she toyed with the long knitting-needles on the work-table.

Some women passed through the yard with a basket of wet clothes.

When she saw them through the window, she suddenly remembered her own wash; as she had soaked it the day before, she must go and rinse it now. So she arose and left the room.

Her tub and her board were on the bank of the Toucques. She threw a heap of clothes on the ground, rolled up her sleeves and grasped her bat; and her loud pounding could be heard in the neighbouring gardens. The meadows were empty, the breeze wrinkled the stream, at the bottom of which were long grasses that looked like the hair of corpses floating in the water. She restrained her sorrow and was very brave until night; but, when she had gone to her own room, she gave way to it, burying her face in the pillow and pressing her two fists against her temples.

A long while afterward, she learned through Victor's captain, the circumstances which surrounded his death. At the hospital they had bled him too much, treating him for yellow fever. Four doctors held him at one time. He died almost instantly, and the chief surgeon had said:

"Here goes another one!"

His parents had always treated him barbarously; she preferred not to see them again, and they made no advances, either from forgetfulness or out of innate hardness.

Virginia was growing weaker.

A cough, continual fever, oppressive breathing and spots on her cheeks indicated some serious trouble. Monsieur Poupart had advised a sojourn in Provence. Madame Aubain decided that they would go, and she would have had her daughter come home at once, had it not been for the climate of Pont-l'Evêque.

She made an arrangement with a livery-stable man who drove her over to the convent every Tuesday. In the garden there was a terrace, from which the view extends to the Seine. Virginia walked in it, leaning on her mother's arm and treading the dead vine leaves. Sometimes the sun, shining through the clouds, made her blink her lids, when she gazed at the sails in the distance, and let her eyes roam over the horizon from the chateau of Tancarville to the lighthouses of Havre. Then they rested in the arbour. Her mother had bought a little cask of fine Malaga wine, and Virginia, laughing at the idea of becoming intoxicated, would drink a few drops of it, but never more.

Her strength returned. Autumn passed. Félicité began to reassure Madame Aubain. But, one evening, when she returned home after an errand, she met M. Boupart's coach in front of the door; M. Boupart himself was standing in the vestibule and Madame Aubain was tying the strings of her bonnet. "Give me my foot-warmer, my purse and my gloves; and be quick about it," she said.

Virginia had congestion of the lungs; perhaps it was desperate.

"Not yet," said the physician, and both got into the carriage, while the snow fell in thick flakes. It was almost night and very cold.

Félicité rushed to the church to light a candle. Then she ran after the coach which she overtook after an hour's chase, sprang up behind and held on to the straps. But suddenly a thought crossed her mind: "The yard had been left open; supposing that burglars got in!" And down she jumped.

The next morning, at daybreak, she called at the doctor's. He had been home, but had left again. Then she waited at the inn, thinking that strangers might bring her a letter. At last, at daylight she took the diligence for Lisieux.

The convent was at the end of a steep and narrow street. When she arrived about at the middle of it, she heard strange noises, a funeral knell. "It must be for some one else," thought she; and she pulled the knocker violently.

After several minutes had elapsed, she heard footsteps, the door was half opened and a nun appeared. The good sister, with an air of compunction, told her that "she had just passed away." And at the same time the tolling of Saint-Léonard's increased.

Félicité reached the second floor. Already at the threshold, she caught sight of Virginia lying on her back, with clasped hands, her mouth open and her head thrown back, beneath a black crucifix inclined toward her, and stiff curtains which were less white than her face. Madame Aubain lay at the foot of the couch, clasping it with her arms and uttering groans of agony. The Mother Superior was standing on the right side of the bed. The three candles on the bureau made red blurs, and the windows were dimmed by the fog outside. The nuns carried Madame Aubain from the room.

For two nights, Félicité never left the corpse. She would repeat the same prayers, sprinkle holy water over the sheets, get up, come back to the bed and contemplate the body. At the end of the first vigil, she noticed that the face had taken on a yellow tinge, the lips grew blue, the nose grew pinched, the eyes were sunken. She kissed them several times and would not have been greatly astonished had Virginia opened them; to souls like these the supernatural is always quite simple. She washed her, wrapped her in a shroud, put her into the casket, laid a wreath of flowers on her head and arranged her curls. They were blond and of an extraordinary length for her age. Félicité cut off a big lock and put half of it into her bosom, resolving never to part with it.

The body was taken to Pont-l'Evêque, according to Madame Aubain's wishes; she followed the hearse in a closed carriage.

After the ceremony it took three quarters of an hour to reach the cemetery. Paul, sobbing, headed the procession; Monsieur Bourais followed, and then came the principal inhabitants of the town, the women covered with black capes, and Félicité. The memory of her nephew, and the thought that she had not been able to render him these honours, made her doubly unhappy, and she felt as if he were being buried with Virginia.

Madame Aubain's grief was uncontrollable. At first she rebelled against God, thinking that he was unjust to have taken away her child—she who had never done anything wrong, and whose conscience was so pure! But no! she ought to have taken her South. Other doctors would have saved her. She accused herself, prayed to be able to join her child, and cried in the midst of her dreams. Of the latter, one more especially haunted her. Her husband, dressed like a sailor, had come back from a long voyage, and with tears in his eyes told her that he had received the order to take Virginia away. Then they both consulted about a hiding-place.

Once she came in from the garden, all upset. A moment before (and she showed the place), the father and daughter had appeared to her, one after the other; they did nothing but look at her.

During several months she remained inert in her room. Félicité scolded her gently; she must keep up for her son and also for the other one, for "her memory."

"Her memory!" replied Madame Aubain, as if she were just awakening, "Oh! yes, yes, you do not forget her!" This was an allusion to the cemetery where she had been expressly forbidden to go.

But Félicité went there every day. At four o'clock exactly, she would go through the town, climb the hill, open the gate and arrive at Virginia's tomb. It was a small column of pink marble with a flat stone at its base, and it was surrounded by a little plot enclosed by chains. The flower-beds were bright with blossoms. Félicité watered their leaves, renewed the gravel, and knelt on the ground in order to till the earth properly. When Madame Aubain was able to visit the cemetery she felt very much relieved and consoled.

Years passed, all alike and marked by no other events than the return of the great church holidays: Easter, Assumption, All Saints' Day. Household happenings constituted the only data to which in later years they often referred. Thus, in 1825, workmen painted the vestibule; in 1827, a portion of the roof almost killed a man by falling into the yard. In the summer of 1828, it was Madame's turn to offer the hallowed bread; at that time, Bourais disappeared mysteriously; and the old acquaintances, Guyot,

Liébard, Madame Lechaptois, Robelin, old Grémanville, paralysed since a long time, passed away one by one. One night, the driver of the mail in Pont-l'Evêque announced the Revolution of July. A few days afterward a new sub-prefect was nominated, the Baron de Larsonnière, ex-consul in America, who, besides his wife, had his sister-in-law and her three grown daughters with him. They were often seen on their lawn, dressed in loose blouses, and they had a parrot and a negro servant. Madame Aubain received a call, which she returned promptly. As soon as she caught sight of them, Félicité would run and notify her mistress. But only one thing was capable of arousing her: a letter from her son.

He could not follow any profession as he was absorbed in drinking. His mother paid his debts and he made fresh ones; and the sighs that she heaved while she knitted at the window reached the ears of Félicité who was spinning in the kitchen.

They walked in the garden together, always speaking of Virginia, and asking each other if such and such a thing would have pleased her, and what she would probably have said on this or that occasion.

All her little belongings were put away in a closet of the room which held the two little beds. But Madame Aubain looked them over as little as possible. One summer day, however, she resigned herself to the task and when she opened the closet the moths flew out.

Virginia's frocks were hung under a shelf where there were three dolls, some hoops, a doll-house, and a basin which she had used. Félicité and Madame Aubain also took out the skirts, the handkerchiefs, and the stockings and spread them on the beds, before putting them away again. The sun fell on the piteous things, disclosing their spots and the creases formed by the motions of the body. The atmosphere was warm and blue, and a blackbird trilled in the garden; everything seemed to live in happiness. They found a little hat of soft brown plush, but it was entirely moth-eaten. Félicité asked for it. Their eyes met and filled with tears; at last the mistress opened her arms and the servant threw herself against her breast and they hugged each other and giving vent to their grief in a kiss which equalized them for a moment.

It was the first time that this had ever happened, for Madame Aubain was not of an expansive nature. Félicité was as grateful for it as if it had been some favour, and thenceforth loved her with animal-like devotion and a religious veneration.

Her kind-heartedness developed. When she heard the drums of a marching regiment passing through the street, she would stand in the doorway with a jug of cider and give the soldiers a drink. She nursed cholera victims. She protected Polish refugees, and one of them even declared that he wished to marry her. But they quarrelled, for one morning when she returned from the Angelus she found him in the kitchen coolly eating a dish which he had prepared for himself during her absence.

After the Polish refugees, came Colmiche, an old man who was credited with having committed frightful misdeeds in '93. He lived near the river in the ruins of a pig-sty. The urchins peeped at him through the cracks in the walls and threw stones that fell on his miserable bed, where he lay gasping with catarrh, with long hair, inflamed eyelids, and a tumour as big as his head on one arm.

She got him some linen, tried to clean his hovel and dreamed of installing him in the bake-house without his being in Madame's way. When the cancer broke, she dressed it every day; sometimes she brought him some cake and placed him in the sun on a bundle of hay; and the poor old creature, trembling and drooling, would thank her in his broken voice, and put out his hands whenever she left him. Finally he died; and she had a mass said for the repose of his soul.

That day a great joy came to her: at dinner-time, Madame de Larsonnière's servant called with the parrot, the cage, and the perch and chain and lock. A note from the baroness told Madame Aubain that as her husband had been promoted to a prefecture, they were leaving that night, and she begged her to accept the bird as a remembrance and a token of her esteem.

Since a long time the parrot had been on Félicité's mind, because he came from America, which reminded her of Victor, and she had approached the negro on the subject.

Once even, she had said:

"How glad Madame would be to have him!"

The man had repeated this remark to his mistress who, not being able to keep the bird, took this means of getting rid of it.

IV

The Bird

He was called Loulou. His body was green, his head blue, the tips of his wings were pink and his breast was golden.

But he had the tiresome tricks of biting his perch, pulling his feathers out, scattering refuse and spilling the water of his bath. Madame Aubain grew tired of him and gave him to Félicité for good.

She undertook his education, and soon he was able to repeat: "Pretty boy! Your servant, sir! I salute you, Marie!" His perch was placed near the door and several persons were astonished that he did not answer to the name of "Jacquot," for every parrot is called Jacquot. They called him a goose and a log, and these taunts were like so many dagger thrusts to Félicité. Strange stubbornness of the bird which would not talk when people watched him!

Nevertheless, he sought society; for on Sunday, when the ladies Rochefeuille, Monsieur de Houppeville and the new habitués, Onfroy, the chemist, Monsieur Varin and Captain Mathieu, dropped in for their game of cards, he struck the window-panes with his wings and made such a racket that it was impossible to talk.

Bourais' face must have appeared very funny to Loulou. As soon as he saw him he would begin to roar. His voice re-echoed in the yard, and the neighbours would come to the windows and begin to laugh, too; and in order that the parrot might not see him, Monsieur Bourais edged along the wall, pushed his hat over his eyes to hide his profile, and entered by the garden door, and the looks he gave the bird lacked affection. Loulou, having thrust his head into the butcher-boy's basket, received a slap, and from that time he always tried to nip his enemy. Fabu threatened to wring his neck, although he was not cruelly inclined, notwithstanding his big whiskers and tattooings. On the contrary, he rather liked the bird and, out of deviltry, tried to teach him oaths. Félicité, whom his manner alarmed, put Loulou in the kitchen, took off his chain and let him walk all over the house.

When he went downstairs, he rested his beak on the steps, lifted his right foot and then his left one; but his mistress feared that such feats would give him vertigo. He became ill and was unable to eat. There was a small growth under his tongue like those chickens are sometimes afflicted with. Félicité pulled it off with her nails and cured him. One day, Paul was imprudent enough to blow the smoke of his cigar in his face; another time, Madame Lormeau was teasing him with the tip of her umbrella and he swallowed the tip. Finally he got lost.

She had put him on the grass to cool him and went away only for a second; when she returned, she found no parrot! She hunted among the bushes, on the bank of the river, and on the roofs, without paying any attention to Madame Aubain who screamed at her: "Take care! you must be insane!" Then she searched every garden in Pont-l'Evêque and stopped the passers-by to inquire of them: "Haven't you perhaps seen my parrot?" To those who had never seen the parrot, she described him minutely. Suddenly she thought she saw something green fluttering behind the mills at the foot of the hill. But when she was at the top of the hill she could not see it. A hod-carrier told her that he had just seen the bird in Saint-Melaine, in Mother Simon's store. She rushed to the place. The people did not know what she was talking about. At last she came home, exhausted, with her slippers worn to shreds, and despair in her heart. She sat down on the bench near Madame and was telling of her search when presently a light weight dropped on her shoulder—Loulou! What the deuce had he been doing? Perhaps he had just taken a little walk around the town!

She did not easily forget her scare, in fact, she never got over it. In consequence of a cold, she caught a sore throat; and some time afterward she had an earache. Three years later she was stone deaf, and spoke in a very loud voice even in church. Although her sins might have been proclaimed throughout the diocese without any shame to herself, or ill effects to the community, the curé thought it advisable to receive her confession in the vestry-room.

Imaginary buzzings also added to her bewilderment. Her mistress often said to her: "My goodness, how stupid you are!" and she would answer: "Yes, Madame," and look for something.

The narrow circle of her ideas grew more restricted than it already was; the bellowing of the oxen, the chime of the bells no longer reached her intelligence. All things moved silently, like ghosts. Only one noise penetrated her ears: the parrot's voice.

As if to divert her mind, he reproduced for her the tick-tack of the spit in the kitchen, the shrill cry of the fish-vendors, the saw of the carpenter who had a shop opposite, and when the door-bell rang, he would imitate Madame Aubain: "Félicité! go to the front door."

They held conversations together, Loulou repeating the three phrases of his repertory over and over, Félicité replying by words that had no greater meaning, but in which she poured out her feelings. In her isolation, the parrot was almost a son, a lover. He climbed upon her fingers, pecked at her lips, clung to her shawl, and when she rocked her head to and fro like a nurse, the big wings of her cap and the wings of the bird flapped in unison. When clouds gathered on the horizon and the thunder rumbled, Loulou would scream, perhaps because he remembered the storms in his native forests. The dripping of the rain would excite him to frenzy; he flapped around, struck the ceiling with his wings, upset everything, and would finally fly into the garden to play. Then he would come back into the room, light on one of the andirons, and hop around in order to get dry.

One morning during the terrible winter of 1837, when she had put him in front of the fire-place on account of the cold, she found him dead in his cage, hanging to the wire bars with his head down. He had probably died of congestion. But she believed that he had been poisoned, and although she had no proofs whatever, her suspicion rested on Fabu.

She wept so sorely that her mistress said: "Why don't you have him stuffed?"

She asked the advice of the chemist, who had always been kind to the bird.

He wrote to Havre for her. A certain man named Fellacher consented to do the work. But, as the diligence driver often lost parcels entrusted to him, Félicité resolved to take her pet to Honfleur herself.

Leafless apple-trees lined the edges of the road. The ditches were covered with ice. The dogs on the neighbouring farms barked; and Félicité, with her hands beneath her cape, her little black sabots and her basket, trotted along nimbly in the middle of the sidewalk. She crossed the forest, passed by the Haut-Chêne and reached Saint-Gatien.

Behind her, in a cloud of dust and impelled by the steep incline, a mail-coach drawn by galloping horses advanced like a whirlwind. When he saw a woman in the middle of the road, who did not get out of the way, the driver stood up in his seat and shouted to her and so did the postilion, while the four horses, which he could not hold back, accelerated their pace; the two leaders were almost upon her; with a jerk of the reins he threw them to one side, but, furious at the incident, he lifted his big whip and lashed her from her head to her feet with such violence that she fell to the ground unconscious.

Her first thought, when she recovered her senses, was to open the basket. Loulou was unharmed. She felt a sting on her right cheek; when she took her hand away it was red, for the blood was flowing.

She sat down on a pile of stones, and sopped her cheek with her handkerchief; then she ate a crust of bread she had put in her basket, and consoled herself by looking at the bird.

Arriving at the top of Ecquemanville, she saw the lights of Honfleur shining in the distance like so many stars; further on, the ocean spread out in a confused mass. Then a weakness came over her; the misery of her childhood, the disappointment of her first love, the departure of her nephew, the death of Virginia; all these things came back to her at once, and, rising like a swelling tide in her throat, almost choked her.

Then she wished to speak to the captain of the vessel, and without stating what she was sending, she gave him some instructions.

Fellacher kept the parrot a long time. He always promised that it would be ready for the following week; after six months he announced the shipment of a case, and that was the end of it. Really, it seemed as if Loulou would never come back to his home. "They have stolen him," thought Félicité.

Finally he arrived, sitting bolt upright on a branch which could be screwed into a mahogany pedestal, with his foot in the air, his head on one side, and in his beak a nut which the naturalist, from love of the sumptuous, had gilded. She put him in her room.

This place, to which only a chosen few were admitted, looked like a chapel and a second-hand shop, so filled was it with devotional and heterogeneous things. The door could not be opened easily on account of the presence of a large wardrobe. Opposite the window that looked out into the garden, a bull's-eye opened on the yard; a table was placed by the cot and held a washbasin, two combs, and a piece of blue soap in a broken saucer. On the walls were rosaries, medals, a number of Holy Virgins, and a holy-water basin made out of a cocoanut; on the bureau, which was covered with a napkin like an altar, stood the box of shells that Victor had given her; also a watering-can and a balloon, writing-books, the engraved geography and a pair of shoes; on the nail which held the mirror, hung Virginia's little plush hat! Félicité carried this sort of respect so far that she even kept one of Monsieur's old coats. All the things which Madame Aubain discarded, Félicité begged for her own room. Thus, she had artificial flowers on the edge of the bureau, and the picture of the Comte d'Artois in the recess of the window. By means of a board, Loulou was set on a portion of the chimney which advanced into the room. Every morning when she awoke, she saw him in the dim light of dawn and recalled bygone days and the smallest details of insignificant actions, without any sense of bitterness or grief.

As she was unable to communicate with people, she lived in a sort of somnambulistic torpor. The processions of Corpus-Christi Day seemed to wake her up. She visited the neighbours to beg for candlesticks and mats so as to adorn the temporary altars in the street.

In church, she always gazed at the Holy Ghost, and noticed that there was something about it that resembled a parrot. The likeness appeared even more striking on a coloured picture by Espinal, representing the baptism of our Saviour. With his scarlet wings and emerald body, it was really the image of Loulou. Having bought the picture, she hung it near the one of the Comte d'Artois so that she could take them in at one glance.

They associated in her mind, the parrot becoming sanctified through the neighbourhood of the Holy Ghost, and the latter becoming more lifelike in her eyes, and more comprehensible. In all probability the Father had never chosen as messenger a dove, as the latter has no voice, but rather one of Loulou's ancestors. And Félicité said her prayers in front of the coloured picture, though from time to time she turned slightly toward the bird.

She desired very much to enter in the ranks of the "Daughters of the Virgin." But Madame Aubain dissuaded her from it.

A most important event occurred: Paul's marriage.

After being first a notary's clerk, then in business, then in the customs, and a tax collector, and having even applied for a position in the administration of woods and forests, he had at last, when he was thirty-six years old, by a divine inspiration, found his vocation: registrature! and he displayed such a high ability that an inspector had offered him his daughter and his influence.

Paul, who had become quite settled, brought his bride to visit his mother.

But she looked down upon the customs of Pont-l'Evêque, put on airs, and hurt Félicité's feelings. Madame Aubain felt relieved when she left.

The following week they learned of Monsieur Bourais' death in an inn. There were rumours of suicide, which were confirmed; doubts concerning his integrity arose. Madame Aubain looked over her accounts and soon discovered his numerous embezzlements; sales of wood which had been concealed from her, false receipts, etc. Furthermore, he had an illegitimate child, and entertained a friendship for "a person in Dozulé."

These base actions affected her very much. In March, 1853, she developed a pain in her chest; her tongue looked as if it were coated with smoke, and the leeches they applied did not relieve her oppression; and on the ninth evening she died, being just seventy-two years old.

People thought that she was younger, because her hair, which she wore in bands framing her pale face, was brown. Few friends regretted her loss, for her manner was so haughty that she did not attract them. Félicité mourned for her as servants seldom mourn for their masters. The fact that Madame should die before herself perplexed her mind and seemed contrary to the order of things, and absolutely monstrous and inadmissible. Ten days later (the time to journey from Besançon), the heirs arrived. Her daughter-in-law ransacked the drawers, kept some of the furniture, and sold the rest; then they went back to their own home.

Madame's armchair, foot-warmer, work-table, the eight chairs, everything was gone! The places occupied by the pictures formed yellow squares on the walls. They had taken the two little beds, and the wardrobe had been emptied of Virginia's belongings! Félicité went upstairs, overcome with grief.

The following day a sign was posted on the door; the chemist screamed in her ear that the house was for sale.

For a moment she tottered, and had to sit down.

What hurt her most was to give up her room,—so nice for poor Loulou! She looked at him in despair and implored the Holy Ghost, and it was this way that she contracted the idolatrous habit of saying her prayers kneeling in front of the bird. Sometimes the sun fell through the window on his glass eye, and lighted a great spark in it which sent Félicité into ecstasy.

Her mistress had left her an income of three hundred and eighty francs. The garden supplied her with vegetables. As for clothes, she had enough to last her till the end of her days, and she economised on the light by going to bed at dusk.

She rarely went out, in order to avoid passing in front of the second-hand dealer's shop where there was some of the old furniture. Since her fainting spell, she dragged her leg, and as her strength was failing rapidly, old Mother Simon, who had lost her money in the grocery business, came every morning to chop the wood and pump the water.

Her eyesight grew dim. She did not open the shutters after that. Many years passed. But the house did not sell or rent. Fearing that she would be put out, Félicité did not ask for repairs. The laths of the roof were rotting away, and during one whole winter her bolster was wet. After Easter she spit blood.

Then Mother Simon went for a doctor. Félicité wished to know what her complaint was. But, being too deaf to hear, she caught only one word: "Pneumonia." She was familiar with it and gently answered:—"Ah! like Madame," thinking it quite natural that she should follow her mistress.

The time for the altars in the street drew near.

The first one was always erected at the foot of the hill, the second in front of the post-office, and the third in the middle of the street. This position occasioned some rivalry among the women and they finally decided upon Madame Aubain's yard.

Félicité's fever grew worse. She was sorry that she could not do anything for the altar. If she could, at least, have contributed something toward it! Then she thought of the parrot. Her neighbours objected that it would not be proper. But the curé gave his consent and she was so grateful for it that she begged him to accept after her death, her only treasure, Loulou. From Tuesday until Saturday, the day before the event, she coughed more frequently. In the evening her face was contracted, her lips stuck to her gums and she began to vomit; and on the following day, she felt so low that she called for a priest.

Three neighbours surrounded her when the dominie administered the Extreme Unction. Afterwards she said that she wished to speak to Fabu.

He arrived in his Sunday clothes, very ill at ease among the funereal surroundings.

"Forgive me," she said, making an effort to extend her arm, "I believed it was you who killed him!"

What did such accusations mean? Suspect a man like him of murder! And Fabu became excited and was about to make trouble.

"Don't you see she is not in her right mind?"

From time to time Félicité spoke to shadows. The women left her and Mother Simon sat down to breakfast.

A little later, she took Loulou and holding him up to Félicité:

"Say good-bye to him, now!" she commanded.

Although he was not a corpse, he was eaten up by worms; one of his wings was broken and the wadding was coming out of his body. But Félicité was blind now, and she took him and laid him against her cheek. Then Mother Simon removed him in order to set him on the altar.

V

The Vision

The grass exhaled an odour of summer; flies buzzed in the air, the sun shone on the river and warmed the slated roof. Old Mother Simon had returned to Félicité and was peacefully falling asleep.

The ringing of bells woke her; the people were coming out of church. Félicité's delirium subsided. By thinking of the procession, she was able to see it as if she had taken part in it. All the school-children, the singers and the firemen walked on the sidewalks, while in the middle of the street came first the custodian of the church with his halberd, then the beadle with a large cross, the teacher in charge of the boys and a sister escorting the little girls; three of the smallest ones, with curly heads, threw rose leaves into the air; the deacon with outstretched arms conducted the music; and two incense-bearers turned with each step they took toward the Holy Sacrament, which was carried by M. le Curé, attired in his handsome chasuble and walking under a canopy of red velvet supported by four men. A crowd of people followed, jammed between the walls of the houses hung with white sheets; at last the procession arrived at the foot of the hill.

A cold sweat broke out on Félicité's forehead. Mother Simon wiped it away with a cloth, saying inwardly that some day she would have to go through the same thing herself.

The murmur of the crowd grew louder, was very distinct for a moment and then died away. A volley of musketry shook the window-panes. It was the postilions saluting the Sacrament.

Félicité rolled her eyes and said as loudly as she could:

"Is he all right?" meaning the parrot.

Her death agony began. A rattle that grew more and more rapid shook her body. Froth appeared at the corners of her mouth, and her whole frame trembled. In a little while could be heard the music of the bass horns, the clear voices of the children and the men's deeper notes. At intervals all was still, and their shoes sounded like a herd of cattle passing over the grass.

The clergy appeared in the yard. Mother Simon climbed on a chair to reach the bull's-eye, and in this manner could see the altar. It was covered with a lace cloth and draped with green wreaths. In the middle stood a little frame containing relics; at the corners were two little orange-trees, and all along the edge were silver candlesticks, porcelain vases containing sun-flowers, lilies, peonies, and tufts of hydrangeas. This mound of bright colours descended diagonally from the first floor to the carpet that covered the sidewalk. Rare objects arrested one's eye. A golden sugar-bowl was crowned with violets, earrings set with Alençon stones were displayed on green moss, and two Chinese screens with their bright landscapes were near by. Loulou, hidden beneath roses, showed nothing but his blue head which looked like a piece of lapis-lazuli.

The singers, the canopy-bearers and the children lined up against the sides of the yard. Slowly the priest ascended the steps and placed his shining sun on the lace cloth. Everybody knelt. There was deep silence; and the censers slipping on their chains were swung high in the air. A blue vapour rose in Félicité's room. She opened her nostrils and inhaled it with a mystic sensuousness; then she closed her lids. Her lips smiled. The beats of her heart grew fainter and fainter, and vaguer, like a fountain giving out, like an echo dying away;—and when she exhaled her last breath, she thought she saw in the half-opened heavens a gigantic parrot hovering above her head.

A Note About the Author

Gustave Flaubert (1821–1880) was a French novelist who was best known for exploring realism in his work. Hailing from an upper-class family, Flaubert was exposed to literature at an early age. He received a formal education at Lycée Pierre-Corneille, before venturing to Paris to study law. A serious illness forced him to change his career path, reigniting his passion for writing. He completed his first novella, *November*, in 1842, launching a decade-spanning career. His most notable work, *Madame Bovary* was published in 1856 and is considered a literary masterpiece.

A Note from the Publisher

Spanning many genres, from non-fiction essays to literature classics to children's books and lyric poetry, Mint Edition books showcase the master works of our time in a modern new package. The text is freshly typeset, is clean and easy to read, and features a new note about the author in each volume. Many books also include exclusive new introductory material. Every book boasts a striking new cover, which makes it as appropriate for collecting as it is for gift giving. Mint Edition books are only printed when a reader orders them, so natural resources are not wasted. We're proud that our books are never manufactured in excess and exist only in the exact quantity they need to be read and enjoyed.

www.ingramcontent.com/pod-product-compliance
Lightning Source LLC
Chambersburg PA
CBHW020314150626
46552CB00022B/2880